THIN AIR

A Novel

Patricia Rockwood

A heartfelt thankyou to Laura Westrich for jumping in on the last lap and pushing me over the finish line.

Thin Air
Written by Patricia Rockwood

Published by Lines End, LLC.
Copyright © 2024 by Patricia Rockwood, Hayden, Colorado. All rights reserved.

ISBN 979-8-218-54761-5

Cover design and illustrations by Patricia Rockwood.

Book formatting by Spots of Joy, LLC.

1
WHO AM I?

The year his mother died, he married. It was no coincidence. She, the mother, was old, large, unintelligent, and doted on him. She, the wife, was young, large, unintelligent, and doted on him. It was a match made in heaven.

Unfortunately, their marriage was short lived. After a few years of abuse, childbearing, and more abuse, the wife packed her bags, her babies, and his money, and set out to start a new life.

Initially, Gloria missed her husband. In the way that prisoners miss their captors, she mourned his absence. He had been familiar. He had needs to attend to, moods to react to, and a house to maintain. He had been there when once there was no one. Now, however, there was no longer no one. There were children. Two. Clearly it was time to move on. Gloria's need to procreate had been fulfilled. Tradition had been satisfied. Society had been appeased. Living to see thirty was bumped to the head of her list. She secured her safety and received full custody without question.

Gloria truly grieved the loss of her marriage, for about the time it took to travel from the court house steps to the taxi. It was an appropriately brief period. The odd nagging loneliness lasted for a few hours in the evening when she was packing. By the time her bruises healed any veil of remorse had been burned on a pyre of anger. When the smoke cleared she stomped around in the ashes a little longer and sat down on a slightly singed packing box to catch her breath.

"Quis sum Ego?" she might well have asked herself at this point, if she had finished tenth grade Latin, which she hadn't. She didn't finish tenth grade. She did remembered the sum ego part but couldn't piece together the rest. She briefly pondered "Who am I?" instead. Then she moved on to "What am I" and the answer was clear.

Without a husband, Gloria embraced her role as a mother. It was a role she was ill-equipped for and inept at, but it was a role nevertheless. Children gave Gloria a place in society, a respectable raison d'etre, a foot in the door. Motherhood is a gift, she decided. She used it well.

Gloria, in fact, would have been lost without her children. They completed her. Not in an existential sense, but in a fashion sense. They made excellent accessories. She felt naked without them. Better to go without a handbag, she mused, than without a child at her side.

The day Chloe was born, Gloria, then relatively meek and soft spoken, had a revelation, the "Aha Moment" of a lifetime.

"Eureka," she said to herself, or something similar, "I look astoundingly good as a mother. Look at the size of my breasts."

She bitterly regretted the effects of bottle feeding. When Hal came along three years later, she nursed him forever, just to maintain the benefit of outstanding cleavage. That was only the beginning.

Whenever she went out, Gloria made sure her children complimented her. She had an unusual, innate artistic sense which she honed in only a few short years into a skill of admirable proportions. She used it to compose scenes even for strangers and bystanders. She was always aware of each of her children's physical relationship to her and to other objects like trees, benches, or any expensive automobiles in the vicinity. She studied magazine pictures and learned to set her son on the wall to her right while positioning her daughter in front of her to the left, thereby reducing the visible width of her hips. Most mothers would stand this way out of warmth and affection for their children. Gloria did it out of a fashion sense. It worked better than vertical stripes. Once she got the hang of lines and shapes she moved on to colors.

Secure in the realm of appearances, Gloria wasn't particularly worried about other aspects of being a single mother. She had strong instincts for survival, and, of course, for other things, too. After surveying herself closely and assessing her situation, from both front and behind, she lost a few pounds, (not many); plucked her eyebrows, (not much); and concluded that though she was no longer young, she was still young-ish. What she needed now was a plan.

Unfortunately, planning wasn't easy for Gloria. She had rarely planned anything in her life, not her marriage, not her children, and certainly not her future in general. She had never really had enough hope to plan anything. With resignation she had simply accepted or rejected whatever came her way.

She was, nevertheless, determined to learn. She contemplated her past. Except for a few high school indiscretions; in the backs of parked cars, under bushes, in elevators, and on pool tables, she had been a good girl. She still had standards. She wouldn't stand around in bars, she wouldn't get a job, and adult education was out of the question.

Divine intervention was required. She attended church diligently in hopes that Jesus Christ would show her the light. If he answered her prayers the light would be shining on a new husband, preferably one who would watch the children while she shopped, an activity that had been sorely lacking during her previous life.

In anticipation of her carefree future, she began shopping like mad. Mostly she shopped for ensembles to wear to church. Dragging her small children from store to store, up and down elevators, and in and out of dressing rooms, she was a woman possessed. Her goal? To be the most seductive woman who ever graced the communion rail. Her ruby lips would match the syrupy, sweet, red wine dripping from them. Her delicate pink tongue, stretching slowly toward the little white wafer, would be painfully attractive to the kneeling gentlemen waiting in anticipation further down the communion line. Her ample bosoms, aided by the Dawn of Synthetic Material, would burst up and out, in a performance designed to force the most respectable gentleman to sit with his hat in his lap.

That winter she wore polka dots, black on white. She preferred narrow waisted dresses (though hers wasn't) with low necklines. Then it was polka dots, black on pink, spattering rayon dresses with double spaghetti straps (a good idea considering the job they had to do). After that it was polka dots, black on yellow, flung across low backed dresses with clinging outlines (not a good idea considering those little bulges). The pattern was clear.

On the outside, however, she wore a plain, gray, calf length, wool coat with a black velveteen collar and matching purse and gloves. Her veneer was both reserved and stylish. She was like a surprise package. Every time she took off her coat everyone was surprised, every time. And mortified. Except for those who were delighted.

The latter category included bored husbands, alter boys, and winos in off the street, hoping to stay warm. It also included unmarried men whose burning desire to attend church was more secular than holy. In their search for the divine they found the sublime, in a sort of trashy, low-class way. Sometimes that's all it takes, particularly on Sunday morning, on a bleak, snowy day in the Midwest in 1959.

2
GLORIA

Winters are long in the Midwest, giving you a lot of time to wish you were elsewhere. The western states are largely populated by first generation Midwesterners who escaped by the skin of their teeth. Some make it as far as the west coast, their origins lost in the anonymity of the masses. Those left behind dig their heels in and bare their teeth at any observations made in retrospect by those who have migrated. The absentees deny any backward longing in the exaggerated fashion of those in denial. Usually what they miss is summers at the lakes, as opposed to the winters at 40 degrees below zero.

In truth, the temperate zone is rarely temperate. It tends to fluctuate wildly from extraordinarily hot to extraordinarily cold. In winter the heavens horde sunlight as if it's storehouses were running low, rationing it out meagerly in midday. Cabin fever, now known as seasonal affective disorder, was once the most common reason isolate Midwest farmers blasted their families into oblivion and voluntarily followed rather than face flat fields of glaring white by day and the black of night by 4 pm. An acronym like SAD doesn't begin to accurately describe the phenomena.

If you live in Chicago, winters are particularly cold, wet, windy and icy, making the summer at the lake portion of the equation even more essential. For Chicagoans the lake factor was Michigan. Chicago's more affluent cruised north in the summer to the forested northern Michigan shores. Their children ran barefoot down the Sleeping Bear Sand Dunes while their parents golfed. They skinny dipped in the evenings on empty shores and ferried to Mackinac

Island to picnic during the day. Vast white sand beaches burned their tender feet. The air along the shores and inner lakes and rivers smelled of pine and occasionally of bonfires.

Gloria had never experienced the smell of summer pine and bonfires. At seventeen Gloria had never left the city. When temperatures hit the nineties she walked to Halsted Street and climbed the stairs to the wooden platform where she inserted her change into the Chiclets dispenser and chewed her gum while waiting for the El. Alena and Katja got on at the next stop. After passing station after station of billboards of mustachioed women and men recently decorated with pointed ears and fangs they continued on foot through the last of the tall buildings where serious downtown Chicago transitioned into the suburbs. In a world of automobiles, concrete and glass temperatures rose exponentially. Every surface exuded heat.

When she and her girlfriends stepped out of the city, somewhere near the North Shore, they were no longer Varvara, Alena and Katja; they were Gloria, Nikki and Katy. They left their Slavic roots and Slavic accents on the train and became the Anglo-Americans they had always wished they had been.

On this stretch of the North Shore the beaches were strips of sand and gravel maybe 25 feet deep, and were occasionally dotted with glass and trash from both picnickers and industry. The water was frigid. A quick splish-splash in the gentle waves provided an instant reprieve from the heat.

Families enjoyed day trips to these beaches and were home for dinner. Young singles and couples stayed longer. Rarely straying too far from the crowd, they engaged in all the hot summer night rituals known to the species since Adam and Eve shared the apple on the beaches of Eden.

GLORIA

Tethered by summer employment Gloria's beach time was limited. She and her friends covered each other with a homemade concoction of baby oil mixed with iodine to enhance their tans and produce the effect of having all the time in the world to lounge about on the sand. If their general appearance occasionally tended to lean a little to the orange end of the spectrum they pretended not to notice.

The girls lay on their towels gossiping and flirting the afternoon away. Periodically they waded through the other beach goers to cool off in the water, stretch their legs and make sure they were highly visible. Once they had turned an acceptable number of heads, they strolled back to their blankets.

Now Gloria drove to the beach in the red and white 1957 Chevy Bel Aire Coupe she gave herself as a divorce present. When she arrived she usually lay alone. Her girlfriends had moved on to other lives and other pastimes. Some no longer needed to provoke instant tans but had the time to nurse the real thing. A few forwent the tanning ritual in favor of kid's baseball games and birthday parties. Most were too tired from picking up a night shift to even think of getting up and heading for the water. They had all moved on.

But Gloria, fully exposed to the sun, refused to step into the light. Like a ghost searching for something lost or misplaced, Gloria once again visited her former haunt. She unfurled dimpled arms and legs on her over-sized terry towel. She coyly adjusted her straps and took note of the people around her.

After her initial assessment, Gloria was oddly unconcerned with the other beach goers. For once, Gloria was oblivious to the impression she may or may not have made on those around her. Gloria was not here to make an impression. She was not here to attract men. She was not here to belong to a crowd. She was not even here to acquire a tan. She was here simply because she could be. At the end of the day, after she had wound her way back through the tall buildings, parked the car in the garage, picked up her kids and lay in bed for the night, Gloria felt like somebody who, after years of doing just what was required of her, finally had a choice.

3

HALLELUJAH

"The blue dress, Chloe, the blue one," Gloria shouted as she dragged Hal down the hallway to the bathroom, his tie and jacket over her shoulder, his chubby little 4-yearold hand clutched in her hand.

"I'm in the pink," she continued, "you have to wear the blue. Matches my eyes."

"And don't forget the hat," she continued shouting even louder over the running water, "they're Episcopal."

"Ouch," Chloe thought sleepily, "not the hat." It had metal clasps that grabbed her in the temples until she wanted to scream.

They had tried a different church every Sunday since Gloria decided to search for salvation. Most of them had been pretty run of the mill and most of them spoke English, at least part of the time. There had been two where no one spoke English before, during or after the service. Gloria acknowledged that these had been poor choices, but at least she had the good manners to stay until they had been dismissed by the clergy. It was only the one with the snakes that had resulted in an immediate retreat. Actually that was the only one to really catch Chloe or Hal's interest. No accounting for taste, Chloe decided.

Gloria rarely made breakfast and never on Sundays. That way she could bribe Hal into silence with a candy bar at the beginning of the sermon. Chloe made herself some toast and took a hard boiled egg from the frig. At nine she was too old to fall for the chocolate routine. An upset stomach before noon didn't appeal to her. Once she had tried to slip Hal a peanut butter sandwich before they got to the church but he told on her and got extra chocolate instead. Every kid for himself, she decided after that.

"Come on, Chloe. Places!" Gloria shouted from the back door. "You're holding us up."

Chloe slipped into the coat that matched her mother's, except for her own plain collar, and met the other two inside the back door, the location of the only family ritual they had ever observed. Here Gloria had mounted the biggest mirror she could find on any of the shopping sprees they had ever been on. Whenever they had an occasion to leave the house together, Chloe and her brother met Gloria at this spot for final adjustments and staging instructions.

"OK. Chloe, you're wearing the blue, so if you can manage it, stand on the step above me, close, to reflect my eyes. Keep your coat unbuttoned and open or it will be pointless. Show that blue!"

"Hal, You stand on the same step with me, but squeeze to the inside of the step. That way when I turn my calf out it will look great from below. If you should happen to innocently grab my skirt and pull it up a little when single men come by there will be something in it for you. I've got a chocolate cherry for you if you get it right the first time without being told. Understand?"

Hal nodded, already tugging at his tie.

"Stop that," said Gloria, pulling his hand away from his neck.

"And Chloe, put these tissues in your pocket and clean him up when he needs it. They'll ruin my line if I put them in mine."

She scrutinized them as a group in the mirror, trying to visualize them on the steps outside the church congenially greeting other worshipers with false familiarity as they approached. The weather was mild for March, a slight breeze would toss her hair, making it sparkle in the morning sun. There would be some early daffodils blooming under the windows behind her against the warmth of the building. Satisfied she turned and opened the backdoor causing them to all scrunch together in the tiny entry way as they exited.

The metal storm door slammed behind them. Her red Chevelle, painstakingly buffed and polished the day before by the boy down the street, was waiting three steps away. Gloria waited behind the wheel while Chloe and Hal climbed in the back seat where they wouldn't muss her.

"Sit still and don't wrinkle," Gloria instructed as she backed out of the driveway.

They drove three miles to the church, during which Gloria repeated her original instructions two more times. Their destination was in a neighborhood that reflected not who Gloria was but who she intended to be. It was a church she hoped not only to be married in but a church she looked forward to being married into.

This church had not been chosen simply because Gloria expected the descendants of the English to be monied, though this was certainly a consideration, it was chosen for its size and the size of everything around it. The houses were big, the yards were big, the trees were big and the cars were big. Even the driveways were big and some had that lovely horseshoe shape so you never had to back up. The very big church was built of very big blocks of grey stone and had a very, very big set of stone steps leading up to an enormous arched doorway set with gigantic oak doors carved with magnificent angels and cherubs.

Gloria's timing was perfect. They were among the first to arrive allowing them to park the car directly in front of the church. She swung across the center line and doubled back in order to park with the driver's side next to the curb, facilitating the show of leg and ankle to anyone interested, as she adjusted herself behind the wheel upon departure.

There, alone on the front steps, stood the minister. Gloria's heart raced with pleasure to see her chosen spot next to him still void of parishioners.

Her vision narrowed. She could see another family coming up the walk.

"Out of the car, now!" she ordered.

Chloe and Hal leaped out of the car.

"Hands!" she barked.

Hal grabbed Gloria's hand. Chloe grabbed Hal's.

The little group scurried past the main sidewalk just in time to be the first to stroll serenely up the walk toward the church. The minister extended his hand towards her as Gloria ascended the stairway.

"Oh so happy," he chimed, "to have you and your charming children visiting God's home away from home this fine spring morning...Hoping to stay?... How can we help... Allow me to introduce you to... "

It was a go.

Gloria retraced her steps by two in order to better point out the daffodils to Mrs. Armbruster, who was arriving just behind her. There she stayed, with her children clustered around her, as choreographed, until the great bells called the congregation to prayer.

Once inside the building Gloria, master of improvisation, put her creativity to work. The mental notes were piling up:

- Families with children towards the back, on the right, for easy bathroom access down the stairs.
- Elderly men and women toward the front to accommodate failing hearing.
- Single women with their parents in the middle, on both sides, with the father respectfully aisle-side.
- Single men in the rear, to the left, near the door, for an easy exit.

It was a predictable pattern that held for most of the churches they had visited. How convenient. No improvisation required.

"Same setup," Gloria whispered to her children. "Hustle now."

They all headed to the very front of the family-with-children section, conveniently opposite the single gentlemen section, so that all the men could see Gloria before them sitting aisle-side as head of her family. Occasionally, when the congregation rose in exaltation to sing a rousing hymn, she would step outside the end of the pew, making her silhouette wholly visible. Once she even knocked her purse to the floor as she returned to her seat, forcing her to lean very far over to retrieve it. She took that moment to look up adoringly at the beautiful windows before sliding back to her place. It was a gesture that fell on grateful eyes.

Gloria had taken note of the number of well-dressed single men near the door. This was a church they would certainly revisit, she thought to herself contentedly.

After the service Gloria paid considerable attention to the comfort of her young offspring and leaned into her car with her derriere facing the departing congregation. She stood up and placed her bag on the hood of the car as she searched for a fictitious item in her purse, then bent again into the back seat of the car. After repeating this maneuver as many times as she thought plausible, Gloria shut the car door, turned toward the church, and in one final gesture, bent forward to pick up a pencil that had strategically fallen into the gutter. Satisfied with her performance, Gloria smiled graciously and waved good-bye to the minister now standing on the grass with a bevy of young men enjoying the fresh scent of spring in the air.

All the way home, Gloria smiled exuberantly and commended her children on their behavior. In the back of her mind she was planning the color of her living room furniture and counting the number of guests she would fit at her dining room table. She was torn between the green and cream pin-striped settee with matching chairs and end tables, and the full-sized floral couch with big, poofy pillows that complimented the reclining chair of her dreams.

She was glancing at each house within two or three blocks of the church, wondering which one would be hers when Hal urgently begged her to stop the car. He threw open the door and chocolate vomit projected all the way across the perfectly manicured boulevard in front of the colonial mansion. Chloe produced the tissues her mother had entrusted to her earlier in the morning and they all continued safely home.

∞

Gloria's hunting grounds had been decided upon. Sunday after Sunday, all through March and into April, Chloe sat in the increasing heat and humidity of the Episcopal Church with the droning of the liturgy washing over her. Occasionally she dropped to her knees with the other parishioners onto the hard leather benches and reached her elbows upward to perch them on the backs of the seats in front of her. Then she rose and incomprehensibly mouthed words that the others seemed to know by heart.

This Sunday the church was half empty. The Easter Sunrise Service had stolen a sizable portion of the congregation, who were now back in bed. Chloe was thankful she had been spared that event. Apparently, her mother thought it unproductive in terms of her personal religious goals.

Chloe twisted uncomfortably in her seat trying to relieve the abrasive effect of the crisp, new dotted Swiss rubbing against her from neck to knees. To her horror her mother had dressed her for Easter in what she had perceived as a stylish junior version of herself. Gloria had been disappointed to find that the smaller dress didn't come in pink with black spots or even black with yellow spots so she purchased it, much to Chloe's relief, in baby blue. Nevertheless, the unfortunate fashion statement made by combining that particular choice of material with the smocking across the chest and the ruffled sleeves trimmed with lace said toddler with hormonal imbalance. Chloe was almost glad she had no friends so they wouldn't see her looking like this.

To her right Hal, genetic recipient of large adenoids, was snoring loudly. The melted chocolate smeared on his mouth and hands had migrated to the cuffs and collar of his excessively crisp, white, dress shirt. Above him loomed the big yellow window of Christ the Shepherd surrounded by children rather than sheep. The Lord's yellow tresses draped gently over his robes as, with staff in hand, he lovingly led his little lambs down a path of daffodils.

To her far left, across the narrow, crimson, carpeted aisle, another bigger and more serious Christ prayed upward in anguish at a rock alter bathed in the deepest reds, blues, and purples. Light streamed down from the glass dramatically mottling the worshipers below in blood and royalty.

Directly next to Chloe, between herself and the dramatic scene farther off, sat her mother and Larry. Larry began eyeing her mother from across the aisle three weeks earlier. It didn't take him long to make his way to his present position. He was a big man and melted in the heat to conform to the pew. His red forehead and prickly pink neck dripped sweat onto the collar of his starchy white shirt. One pudgy hand lay tensely over her mother's stockinged knee. The other lay uncomfortably in the lap of his grey tweedy trousers. His eyes strained to look forward but kept straying back to her mother's bosom, which rose and fell more deeply under their scrutiny.

The minister was booming something about not being fit to eat crumbs. "Amen" echoed throughout the church. There was more about sins and transgressions and bones wasting away. It ended in rejoicing and resurrection. Chloe had weeks earlier given up trying to make any sense of it on her own. She only stared up at the alter and followed along in the books to distract herself from her mother's activities. Occasionally she bellowed out hymns with the rest of the congregation to help the period of her captivity pass more quickly.

Larry sluggishly shifted his weight from one side to the other and back again before finally deciding to remove his suit jacket and lay it across his lap. Her mother's hand slowly slid up his leg and under it. Larry sweated more than ever.

Suddenly the organ brought the congregation abruptly to its feet and the recession began. Stepping in time with oppressively heavy hosannas played at a criminally slow pace everyone filed to the back of the church and down the stairs to the undercroft. Larry escorted Gloria while Chloe and Hal fumbled along after, unable to see anything higher than belts and behinds. Jumping blindly into this river of people in hopes of reaching a safe destination was the greatest test of faith required of anyone in the building that day.

Halfway down the stairs the deep hosannas disappeared in an airy cloud of tiny voices singing "All things bright and beautiful…" as the Sunday school came to a close. In the basement of the church children whose parents had enrolled them earlier in the year were putting away their papers and crayons. Women brought out cookies and coffee, and began laying plates and napkins on the table to serve the Easter cake, a holiday specialty with a single dime baked inside. The receiver of the prized dime laden piece would be blessed with a year's good luck.

Chloe went to the kitchen and without hesitation tore her ludicrous white Easter bonnet from her head and quickly stuffed it behind the coffee machine. Thoughts of retrieving it never entered her head. With a complete change of momentum, she moved as slowly as possible, delaying the moment when she would have to go back into the common room. Even after five Sundays, it was still a room filled with strangers. She helped herself to a glass of water and sipped it. Two women preparing trays of food exchanged sympathetic looks for the mentally impaired little girl who took five minutes to work the kitchen faucet and another five to wander around the room examining drawers and cupboards before finding the door.

After weeks and weeks of church hopping, Chloe had learned not to form any Sunday morning attachments. It was painful, pointless, and more often than not, extremely humiliating. She had decided to patiently wait for her mother to get over her Episcopal infatuation and move onto something more ecumenical, a word she looked up the previous week and tried to use in a sentence at least three times.

Hot, tired and completely intimidated, Chloe climbed up to the back of a sturdy wooden bench and perched with her back against the wall, nearly disappearing in a pile of choir robes. She saw her mother hasten down the hallway, past the coats and jackets hanging there, and turn left into the ladies room. She watched as Hal fooled around with the other boys waiting for their cake. They chased each other up and down the stairs and wrestled each other to the floor repeatedly until one adult after another, with a display of artificial Sunday morning patience, tried to calm them down.

Tedium was winning, Chloe was getting drowsy. Her mind was drifting off. She half noticed sweaty Larry heading for the men's room, but instead he also turned left and followed her mother. Her eyelids drooped as Hal grabbed his cake and stuffed it in his mouth. He started to cough. The boys laughed. The more he coughed and flailed his arms, the more they laughed. His face was very red as he hit the floor. There was a strange silence and then all hell broke loose. Chloe leaped up, wide awake now, but she could only watch as people shook Hal, yelled at Hal, and vainly thumped on Hal's back.

Someone shouted for her mother and Chloe ran to the bathroom, where in his urgency, fat Larry had turned left into the ladies' room where her mother waited. In his haste he had neglected to lock the door. Try as she might, Chloe was never able to erase the picture of Larry with his boxers around his ankles and her mother seated on the bathroom sink.

That was the day Hal got the lucky dime and Chloe learned a bout everlasting life.

4
GOOD-BYE HAL

Hal's funeral came and went before Chloe had a chance to comprehend that he was gone. She and her mother were moved to the first row of the Episcopal Church in order to be closer to the coffin and to the heartfelt condolences and blessings which rained down upon them from the pulpit that loomed up directly before them. Chloe vainly wished she were still wearing the formerly detestable baby blue, dotted Swiss with the white Easter bonnet instead of the black velvet with the starchy, black veil.

The funeral was small and existed at all only by the good graces of the Ladies' Auxiliary, who took it upon themselves to sit together in the back of the church in a show of support and solidarity. Fortunately, their gossiping tongues could not be heard as far as the front row of pews. Their whisperings revealed far much less sympathy for the bereaved mother than sympathy for the children born to such a slut. They traced the shame of her behavior much farther back than the inexcusable episode in the washroom.

Although King James had long ago included divorce in in relation to his version of the bible, the vast majority of this particular branch of his descendants still considered it, if not a mortal sin, then at least a social one, which should be born entirely on the shoulders of the faithless wife. The congregational fruit does not fall far from the tree, which in this case would be Catholic. If Gloria had remained married every one of them would have rallied behind her and berated her husband mercilessly for his treatment of her. They would have looked with horror on her bruised arms and back. They would have told her she was a saint as long as she covered those offending marks with conservative, moderately perky double knit and held her head high in church. They would have urged her to leave the sadist forthwith. However, since she had actually done just that of her own volition, she was forever doomed in their eyes to the position of the selfish harpy who put her own lascivious needs above those of her poor children and slaving husband. In their opinion, all her heartbreak was simply the inevitable result of her initial and inexcusable course of action, divorce. It was doubly offensive that she had managed to become a smiling convivial divorcee who absolutely glowed with animal magnetism. Better she should have become a lonely, frustrated, shriveled, old hag deserving of their sympathy.

In due course, the conversation turned to Chloe, the odd, silent, mentally impaired child who had been observed wandering aimlessly about the undercroft on numerous occasions. One hated to use the word "retarded" but clearly she must be. They imagined the trials of her sad little fatherless life, never once considering how much better off Chloe had been without him. The overall mood changed and sympathy for Gloria was finally kindled when they began to construct a life where poor Gloria was able to wear a happy face even though shackled with a crazy daughter. And such a pretty little thing too. That would make life even more complicated. Oh, the problems that lay ahead. Could you really allow people like that to reproduce?

When they tired of talking, and it wasn't quickly, all eyes turned forward to the pitifully small coffin and the two solitary figures before it. They thought of their own lives and pictured, though try as they might not to, the outlines of their own children in the same circumstance. Even the most coldhearted of them cried, though more for themselves than for Hal. Eventually they cried for Chloe, and for Gloria by association.

The service was relatively brief. The head of the Ladies' Auxiliary, who had driven them to the service, returned Chloe home afterwards and sat with her while her mother went on to the cemetery with the minister. The woman considered Chloe's disabilities, which clearly must include impaired hearing and absent vocal chords, and spoke to her very loudly in sentences of no more than three or four words accompanied by a lot of gesticulation, all of which made her very hard to understand. Speculating on how long it would be before the youngster had to be institutionalized, she tried her best not to antagonize the child for fear she might become violent. The girl was small, but crazy people were known to sometimes possess superhuman strength. She cautiously backed away from Chloe.

That's when Chloe finally cried. Who was this woman who shouted incomprehensibly and waved her arms about from the far corner of the room? Why had she been left on this day of all days to care for a lunatic. When would her mother come home. Would her mother ever come home at all?

Chloe turned and ran up the stairs and into the safety of her room. Locking the door securely behind her she scanned the recesses of her room for anything suitable to add to her string of bed sheets, which were the first step in her plan of eventual escape to anywhere far, far away ¬¬ possibly Rome or New South Wales. Last time she had connected them they were still 11 feet short of reaching the ground. She tore the sheets from her bed and tied them end to end as fast as possible. She added two jump ropes to the string and fell onto her bed with her atlas in hand. She couldn't wait until she was twelve, she had to make a run for it now.

The back door slammed. Muffled voices could be heard coming from the kitchen. Gloria was home.

Chloe began to cry all over again. Then she fell asleep.

5
ALONE

In the days following Hal's funeral one might think Chloe would have become infinitely more precious to Gloria, but it was quite the opposite. In her grief for her son, Gloria quite forgot her daughter. Gloria was oblivious to anything but herself.

Larry disappeared in a heartbeat engulfed in a cloud of ostracism and distaste. Rumor had it that he had embraced the teachings of Martin Luther and was wooing a middle-aged Scandinavian woman at a church ten blocks over. The sturdily built woman was heiress to several lucrative farms in northern Minnesota and needed someone who could help her manage them. Apparently, he and Gloria had been playing the same game.

Chloe was left to herself to sort out her own feelings. Hal had been more a part of her mother's life than of her own. Hal had been her mother's best prop. Gloria usually left the house in the morning with Hal in tow and Chloe sent herself off to school. Gloria took Hal with her to the park when she wanted to look young and sporty. Chloe had outgrown that niche. Gloria took Hal window shopping even in the coldest weather, thinking he might make a good conversation piece. Chloe was clearly not fit for that role. Gloria had always intended to take Chloe out of the closet after she had established a solid relationship with a man. In the meantime, Hal had been her mother's only child.

As a result of their separation, Chloe did not really miss Hal, not as a person anyway. He was missed more as an event, something that went on around you, like the passage of a train or the sound of a vacuum cleaner. A little piece of the texture of life was gone. It made her unhappy, but not inconsolable.

For several days the house was filled with strangers pretending to be friends. Chloe tried to find herself a place in the melee but shortly discovered she could not keep opening the door to sad, sympathetic faces attached to dinner entrees, flowers and assorted ferns. She picked up her sweater and slipped out the back door unnoticed.

The sun had broken through the clouds long enough to evaporate the morning rain from the grass. She lay face up in the back yard next to the driveway and gazed at the sky, examining the full circle of her vision. Trees, house, garage; nothing had changed. It all lay flat against the blue-white of a humid sky that never quite cleared. She took her time and considered it all in detail. Big flakes of grey paint were peeling from the side of her house. The remains of last year's sparrow's nests poked out from under the eaves. Above her, black branches and lacy oak leaves swayed gently in the breeze making the light sparkle as it passed through. The sunny side of the garage where the ladder hung leaned slightly to the right. Occasionally a squirrel ran across the roof on its way to the next telephone wire.

Chloe didn't dwell on the house, it held too much confusion. The garage, however, was something else. Formerly a barn, later a carriage house, the crumbling structure now housed her mother's car and a large variety of unused tools, old lawnmowers and decomposing lumber. Rising from the cracked concrete floor, nearly invisible against the rear wall, was a wooden ladder to the loft. Last summer Chloe secretly ventured up to the attic and looked out of the hayloft at the surrounding neighborhood. Now she longed for that feeling of height, the view from above, unseen and unobserved. She wanted to distance herself from the earth. Even at nine Chloe needed to look out at Beyond.

In no time she was at the top of the ladder. There she paused. She was unconcerned with the fact that her presence here was forbidden, but she was aware that it was dangerous. The brightness from the small open loft doors across the room did not illuminate the space. On the contrary, the brightness there made the rest of the room and its contents nearly indistinguishable in comparison. Chloe's desire to feel her way across the room was countered by her wariness of what she might feel.

No hay from years long past remained in the loft. Now it housed primarily forgotten storm windows with cracked and broken panes, and several inches of thick, gray dust mixed with spider webs. Shards of broken glass lay everywhere. Chloe stopped to collect a few and hold them up to the small, nearly tangible beams of light that entered through cracks in the walls and ceiling. She flinched as she cut herself and became momentarily absorbed in the striking way the red of her blood left a path in the grey dirt on the glass, then dripped to the floor making pock marks in the dust. The air was dry and stale. Her throat and lungs yearned for relief. Footprints followed her as she advanced cautiously across the floor. It sunk ominously in response to the passing of even Chloe's small frame.

She bent over and stepped out of the loft doors onto the roof where she stood for a moment in the sun just outside the door. She paused, not unseen and hidden, but upright in full view of anyone who might look up. She stood there in a childishly arrogant way, briefly confident that no one would. Then she slipped off her shoes and socks in order to better grip the wooden shingles with her toes She crouched down for better balance and increased anonymity, and made her way across the front of the building and around to the side, out of obvious view. Tennis shoes in hand, she headed for the far end of the roof where the lilac bushes covered the corner of the building.

Looking back to where she had traveled Chloe was surprised that she had successfully completed the trip. From this vantage point the missing and crumbling shingles were more visible, as were the slippery mossy patches which were more often hidden from the sun. She took a moment to turn a full circle with her head above the bushes, inhaling the greenery and absorbing the view. Then she sat down and disappeared completely in the budding foliage.

Her finger was still bleeding. She found a tissue in her pocket and carefully folded it accordion style, wrapped it around her little finger and tied it carefully in a knot, neatly tucking in the ends. Satisfied with her work, she parted a few branches, rested her chin on her knees, and gazed out at the world.

Chloe was still at an age when thoughts present themselves as often in feelings as they do in words. Her thoughts now filled her whole being and disappeared into her subconscious. Soon she would unwittingly enter upon a lifetime of squeezing and pruning experiences into words and sentence structure that others could comprehend, diminishing the fullness of her life in the process. Unaware of the narrowing of the path of her reality, Chloe sat feeling no regret for her pending loss or any foreboding for her future. She sat not in a state of childish simplicity but in a state of richness and complexity she may not often have again.

The afternoon passed softly and simply. At first, she watched a beetle crawl over her bare toes and around her shoes, hurrying to get wherever he was going or to get away from wherever he had come from. A pair of robins was stuffing sticks and fluff into a crook in a lilac branch. She watched the cars go past her house and a few kids playing catch. Their mother ran out and scolded them when they followed their ball into the street.

Chloe rolled her back down onto the roof and rested her head on her socks, which, theoretically, would keep the beetles out of her hair. The sun seeped into her skin and she shut her eyes. She watched the shapes and colors of the light drift across the inside of her eye lids as she descended into sleep.

When the sun began to disappear behind the trees across the street and the air became suddenly several degrees cooler, Chloe awoke with a shiver. She rose and left the roof in the quickest and most direct route, by tossing her shoes over the edge and swinging down a couple of lilac branches to the ground. She was in no hurry as she crossed the lawn to the backdoor. She quietly slipped inside.

No one had missed her. No one asked where she had been. Her mother was sitting alone in the living room by the window in the twilight. Chloe pulled the curtains as she had seen her mother do many times. She turned on a light for her as she passed out of the room and ascended the staircase. Her mother said nothing.

6
METAMORPHOSIS

In all the time Gloria had dragged Hal around for the visual effect it never dawned on her how much she loved him. Now her devastation was all consuming. She really had no idea what was happening to her. In a few brief moments her whole life had changed. She didn't know she was heartsick, she only knew that she was sick. She couldn't eat. She barely slept. She moved about her house like an invalid opening and closing the shades for no particular reason and clutching the backs of chairs for support as she made her way back to the couch.

Having had no experience with grief of this proportion, Gloria wandered from doctor to doctor searching for the cause of her illness. Pharmaceutical cocktails in whopping quantities kept her up in the daytime and asleep at night. Apparently, she had all the stylish mental disorders of the day, depending on which doctor she spoke to. Never having known Gloria before the accident, professionals had a hay-day shaping the clay in their own images. The fact that there was very little "Gloria" left when they were done bothered no one in particular. In fact, more than a few people who knew her before Hal's death secretly liked Gloria better this way.

Only Chloe was disturbed by the difference. Every aspect of life had become unreal. It reminded her of the underwater world of Jacques Cousteau. Her mother drifted about like flotsam suspended a few feet below the sparkling surface of the water where she used to exist and Chloe was pulled along, attached by unseen tendrils of familial bonds. Chloe inevitably felt seasick by noon nearly every day.

Every Tuesday afternoon the currents deposited Chloe and her mother at the doctor's door. Once seated in the faux leather chair between the bowl of hard candies and the box of Kleenex she listened intently as the doctor evaluated, instructed, and adjusted her mother's perceptions and prescriptions. Chloe pressed herself deeply into the cushions of her chair and never said a word. Her attempt at becoming completely invisible was so effective that the doctor never once questioned the appropriateness of her presence in the room. Gloria was ultimately advised to resume her life, to go back to the things she knew and to rely on time and habit, as we all do in times of crisis.

With instructions to take all medications as ordered and to return again the following Tuesday, Chloe and Gloria departed, leaving the sound proof vacuum of the psychiatrist's office behind. Chloe took her mother's hand and helped her through the glass doors and down the hallway back to harsh reality.

The psychiatrist's office was well hidden in the bowels of a commercial building for the purpose of obscuring the comings and goings of the crazy people. It was not yet vogue to exchange the names and numbers of one's therapists or to chat casually at cocktail parties about one's preferred psychoactive drug, legal or otherwise. Society was not yet ready to accept mental disorders as illnesses that can come and go like a bad flu depending on your chemical make-up, level of resistance and degree of exposure. Consequently, the clinic had a respectable front entrance street side between the fashion boutique and the coffee shop and a hidden escape route in the back where patrons could depart unseen without revealing the shame of their bad blood. Chloe and Gloria emerged from the premises through a plain brown door into the parking lot where a cab awaited them.

They were home in time for lunch. The house was empty. Weeks earlier the neighborhood had become tired of its involvement in the tragedy. Well-wishers had had their fill of exhibiting who could be most sympathetic. The bouquets died. The casseroles stopped coming. The cloud of hysteria and concern dissipated. People drifted back home, first one by one then en masse like a flock of flamingos lifting off from a swamp. Now, Chloe was left alone with her mother.

Fixating on the doctor's advice Chloe took it upon herself to coax her mother back to her old habits. As Chloe recalled, this meant shopping, so shop she did. Dragging her mother from store to store, up and down elevators, in and out of dressing rooms Chloe forced her passive and compliant mother to shop. Boutiques, department stores, book stores, hardware stores, any establishment that encouraged perusing shelves, aisles or stacks became part of their rounds. Actual purchases were few. When necessary Gloria paid the cab fare and complacently signed whatever checks Chloe wrote on their diminishing bank account.

What was Chloe's goal? To elicit a familiar response. Chloe was waiting for the day her mother would try to match lipstick to nail polish, shoes to dress, coat to hat. Any act that would indicate that Gloria would someday dress herself in the morning and Chloe could resume her old life, however dissatisfying it had been.

Eventually it began to work. One morning on the third floor of Marshal Fields a tiny glint of recognition appeared in Gloria's eyes. She looked from the dress rack to the mirror and back again repeatedly as if she had once again tapped into the Jungian Flow of Universal Shopping Consciousness. Like an amnesiac remembering details of a former life, Gloria's recovery snowballed. It suddenly dawned on her that she looked stunning in black. Little black velvet hats with tiny black veils perched atop her freshly cropped blonde hair. Short black jackets with black satin collars hugged her newly svelte figure, the stylish by-product of pain and remorse. Snug black skirts that hung just below the knee with a bit of a slit up the side revealed the calves she had always taken pride in. The mourning-and-hysteria diet had paid off. Gloria was back better than ever.

Her recovery was significantly aided by the outcome of the recent lawsuit against St. John's Episcopal Church. The lord finally came through for her. The sun came out, the clouds parted, and the archangel Gabriel himself floated down from heaven with a check sporting six figures. The Episcopal Church carries a lot of weight, but then again so do charges of negligent homicide.

The healing power of wealth is indisputable. It's a proven medical fact that a large influx of cold cash facilitates the action of nearly all varieties of benzodiazepine-based drugs. The onset of action is immediate and the duration lasts a very long time, depending on the amount of cash administered. In Gloria's case an exceptionally extended duration was imminent.

Gloria's former co-parishioners, though bitter, did not go away entirely empty handed. All in all the parish of St. John's Episcopal Church was privileged to bear witness to a real miracle. Before their very eyes Gloria was transformed nearly overnight from "that shameless slut Gloria" to "our own, poor dear Gloria" and back to "that shameless slut Gloria". It was a metamorphosis of biblical proportions.

Gloria, too, had a revelation. She discovered that without the burden of finding a man to support her, her need for God was greatly diminished. This freed up her Sundays for more entertaining activities. Enthusiastically she rescheduled.

Unfortunately, money can't make up for lack of imagination. Gloria went back to reliving her high school days. She returned to parked cars, bushes, elevators and pool tables. More sophisticated women may have become bored with this venue, but not Gloria. Gloria was having a great time.

7
EVILS OF ENNUI / ENTER DENNIS

Eventually, however, Gloria discovered that the 24-hour day is vastly over rated. She was having considerable difficulty filling it. When having a great time didn't last long enough Gloria took Hal's t-shirt out of her top drawer and slept with it on her pillow bunched up against her face. She imagined the softness of his hair. She breathed the scent of him into her dreams. It went back in the drawer the next morning and she went on with her life.

Gloria had been unable to face emptying Hal's room until weeks after he was gone. When she was finally up to the task, there wasn't that much to do. They had only moved into their new house a few months earlier and everything he had grown out of had been disposed of then. Now Gloria packed Hal's remaining belongings into boxes, deciding to save nothing but pictures. The boxes barely filled the trunk of her car. She returned to his room for one last look around, as if she were checking out of a motel. She looked in the empty drawers and the back of the closet. She bent down on her knees and peered under Hal's bed. There, crumpled up in a wad in the corner, were three t-shirts that hadn't made it to the laundry basket.

Gloria pulled the bed away from the wall, intending to throw the shirts out rather than wash and pack them. Instead she sat on the edge of the bed and stared at them. She buried her face in them and inhaled all that was left of Hal.

She took the shirts to the kitchen and wrapped them individually in plastic bags, taping them securely shut so that none of the sweet perfume could escape. They fit discreetly in the back of the top, right hand drawer of Gloria's bureau where they wouldn't confront her unexpectedly but were easily accessible when she really needed them.

She took a quick shower and slipped into something cool and colorful that coordinated well with the car. Then she drove herself to lunch, stopping briefly at the Salvation Army on the way. She nibbled her salad slowly and lingered over her grilled cheese and coke pondering the direction of her life.

The novelty of her promiscuity, though not exactly short-lived, did eventually wear off. By mid-July Gloria's footloose and fancy-free lifestyle was beginning to feel like a heavy responsibility. Money and independence, though initially exhilarating, came with a hitch. As the mist of marital woes and monetary fears evaporated from about her head, Gloria discovered a clarity of mind previously unexplored. Without the timeconsuming focus and agility associated with walking on eggshells for her husband or groveling for strangers attentions in hopes of securing her future, Gloria not only had time to think but found she was capable of doing so. It was both exhilarating and frightening.

From the moment she reached the bottom of the stairs in the morning until she shut her eyes in bed at night Gloria thought. All day long she thought incessantly. It began to be very annoying. She thought about the articles she read in fashion magazines, she remembered recipes she saw in Ladies' Home Journal, she analyzed the movies she watched. Occasionally she read a book or two. In a moment of wild abandon, she even tuned in to the nightly news. She was not satisfied. She needed more.

She looked around for inspiration, but none came. Her close circle of friends was nonexistent as was her list of famous women to emulate. Betsy Ross knew how to sew. Madam Curie had a way with the electron microscope. Gloria had neither of these skills. She vainly searched the recesses of her mind for other famous female legends. In the end Annie Oakley and Dale Evans were all she could muster.

In lieu of inspiration Gloria decided camaraderie might suffice. She longed for a mission, a challenge, the feeling of adrenaline surging through her veins. The only excitement she had had in her husband's house had been life threatening. Excitement inspired by something that didn't leave bruises would be incredibly refreshing.

Gloria was a woman whose spirits would have soared in response to slogans like "Uppity Women Unite!" Unfortunately, the only bumper stickers available for Gloria's edification tended to read "Eat at Joe's bait shop" or "I visited the Corn Palace, S. Dakota". The walls of the ladies' restroom where not scrawled with "Well Behaved Women Rarely Make History". On the contrary, the most common advice Gloria had ever received was, "If you can't say something nice, don't say anything at all".

Vainly Gloria searched for a cause, a big one, something comparable to WWII but veering less toward Armageddon. She had seen old newsreels in which women had eagerly rushed into industry in support of their troops. They absolutely beamed up at the camera in the midst of weapon production. Of course, few women where Gloria had grown up had rushed patriotically to the factories, many were already there. Theoretically, however, it seemed invigorating.

She called for her check and exited the restaurant still dissatisfied, still searching.

Eventually Gloria's dissatisfaction grew into something more than dissatisfaction, her searching, something more than searching. Her clarity of vision extended in all directions revealing little more than the emptiness of her life. Fear hid itself in a gnawing ball in the pit of her stomach. It sat there all day and prevented her from eating. It sat there all night and prevented her from sleeping. It never cried out saying, "here I am, I am Fear, come and conquer me." That type of challenge Gloria might have understood. Instead, fear crept insidiously into every pore of Gloria's body and silently took effect. Her lustrous hair was becoming dull. Her deep-set blue eyes were beginning to appear sunken. Her soft, pink skin was becoming ashen. Something had to be done, if only for the sake of appearances.

Lesser women may have taken to having a nip in the afternoon but at her core Gloria was made of better stuff. She took to spending an afternoon or two at the public library wandering through the stacks. While she was there she considered learning new things. Unfortunately, she lacked guidance, direction and most important company. She went home.

She joined the Great Books Club and attended a few meetings. She actually thought that a couple of the books were great, but the company was mundane. Again, she went home.

One day over coffee with herself in the kitchen Gloria's mind ran away with her. It took her to Paris for croissants and café au lai at a quaint, little street-side cafe where everyone said, "Oui, oui, mademoiselle". It took her to the theater where South Pacific, Oklahoma and Brigadoon played simultaneously. No one talked, everyone sang, no one walked, everyone danced. She sang *Bali Hai* as she rode in a surrey with the fringe on top and all the men wore kilts. It put her on a podium where flags waved, bands played and everyone cheered her name proclaiming her the best, at what it was unclear, but definitely the best. It took her into the arms of Richard Burton, Frank Sinatra, Mickey the policeman and Joe the grocery takeout boy.

By the time she had finished her third cup of coffee Gloria realized it was midafternoon. She was still at the kitchen table and there were many empty hours left to be filled before bedtime. This routine continued for enough days to cause Gloria some serious concern.

Essentially Gloria was bored. She was smart enough to be profoundly bored. Who would have guessed? The maxim that the idol mind is the devil's playground is not to be taken lightly. Boredom is not a thing to be trifled with. It cannot be overcome by keeping your hands busy. It cannot be whisked away with idol conversation. Boredom can be devastating. It can cause Pomeranians to lose their fur. It can incite prison inmates to riot. Combined with isolation and loneliness, it had caused medieval European housewives abandoned daily in their huts in the forests to invent the friendly hearth elves who evolved into the foundations of Satanism, magic, and witchery that led to burning at the stake on a massive scale. It caused Gloria to accept Dennis.

Dennis was essentially Gloria's attempt to return to the norm, sort of like Pepto Bismol for the soul. Unfortunately, her marriage had ended because the norm for Gloria was unacceptable. Nevertheless, Gloria once again achieved some measure of comfort performing the Dance of the Eggshells to an appreciative audience. The atmosphere of her brain regained it's formerly comfortable level of fog and high humidity and the fear in her stomach subsided somewhat, but not entirely.

That little hint of discomfort that remained just below her sternum in the vicinity of her solar plexus was the reason Gloria singled Dennis out of a bevy of suitors for a single, shining attribute. Dennis was married. Gloria knew he was married. Even Chloe knew he was married. She had seen him slide the gold band off his finger one evening and slip it into his pocket before ringing the bell. It was the first unspoken secret Gloria and Chloe ever held between them because Dennis, self-inflated, egomaniacal creature that he was, did not know they knew.

Clearly the best feature of a married man is that he cannot be married. This loophole allowed Gloria to hold on to the hope that someday she might hang up her dance shoes forever. Chloe was able to feel secure in the knowledge that she would never wake up in the morning and find Dennis in the house.

The relationship seemed to work for everyone. Gloria allowed Dennis to woo her. Chloe allowed Dennis to dislike her intensely and pretend he didn't. Dennis behaved as if he were planning a cozy future for the three of them when there wasn't a chance in hell of him following through. It was a superb performance in the tradition of the Japanese shadow play where all that can be seen is the outlines of little paper dolls bouncing around on sticks controlled by unseen hands. The faces on the dolls are never even painted on. Similarly, neither Gloria, Chloe nor Dennis ever revealed their true expressions.

8
ABOVE AND BEYOND

When Chloe felt the envelope of her acting skills being stretched to its outer limit she returned to the lilacs. She adventurously climbed about on the roof top of the garage retrieving thick tenacious clumps of moss and patiently arranging them into a fuzzy green carpet under the branches. She would sit upright or rest her head on a moss pillow while precociously lost in a story by Poe who gave her the shivers or quotes from Thoreau, who reassured her that those who spent their time alone did so because life was better that way.

"It's not that we love to be alone, but that we love to soar, and when we do soar, the company grows thinner and thinner till there is none at all," she read, and life made more sense. Occasionally she ventured to the top of the roof to see if the air tasted any different at the summit or if the thinness of it would make it harder to breathe.

Once, in elementary school, she had come upon a picture of a bust of Pallas Athene in a mythology book. She remembered her now and checked a mythology book out of a nearby public library. Armed with tracing paper and # 2 pencils she climbed the garage ladder with the book tucked in the back of her jeans. She spent an entire afternoon on her moss carpet in the sky drawing copies of Pallas, virgin goddess of wisdom and war and adding the Raven in various positions. She recited throughout, "Prophet! said I, "thing of evil! ...prophet still, if bird or devil!...". Chloe half expected her chant to cause the bird to rise up off the paper and fly around her head several times before mistaking her for the silver-eyed goddess and alighting on her shoulder. She could almost feel his cold, ebony beak nipping at her ear while whispering "Nevermore" deep into her soul.

One afternoon, a Walden Pond afternoon, Chloe arose from her perch to test her altitude. To the east the sky was acquiring a heavy black foreboding appearance. It was separated from the earth only by a deep, smoky haze pierced by long, silvery threads of rain. Chloe stood and watched as an ominous, dark shadow advanced over the landscape toward her.

The storm was still distant when Chloe was engulfed in shimmering rain falling from the clear blue sky directly above her. Entranced in this magical microcosm she tipped her head back slowly and smiled as the tiny drops touched her face. As she did so the moss at her feet, moistened not only by the rain falling from the sky above, but also by the rivulets washing down from higher up on the roof, experienced its own little mud slide, taking Chloe with it. Still looking skyward, Chloe found herself descending in unison with the droplets over the side of the building.

Chloe later remembered a moment of pleasant flight and dreamed about it whenever she could. On a really good night she extended the dream to include a reversal of direction that lifted her up above the roof, then above the house, then above the city where she lived. She rose and dipped and rose again as the storm went on below her.

It was not her mother who found her but the elderly woman who lived next door. She had come out to her garden that evening to search for some late season asparagus to serve with her dinner. She found Chloe hidden in the short forest of green stalks and red berries. Initially, she thought the child had stretched out to nap in the sweet-smelling coolness of the garden after the rain. When she realized the red streaks in her hair were not made by the berries she cried out urgently for her hired man, Jack. He scooped Chloe up in his arms and whisked her into the house.

Chloe awoke to the smell of peonies. She was not alone. Clara Fitz was sitting sipping tea and reading to herself at a desk directly across the room from her. There was a tall narrow vase filled with white peonies next to her. The woman was framed by a variety of photographs and tintypes of little girls in linen dresses and hair bows as big as their heads. Women with tall collars and men sitting seriously in their best suits and reading glasses looked out at her. Babies cooed in their christening dresses. Couples in wedding attire stared unsmiling around the room. Clara's lineage was well represented.

Clara herself was an exact duplicate of the woman in the photograph to the upper right, the one with the two little boys about Chloe's age. A strikingly handsome, darkhaired man stood at her side in front of the photographer's drapes. The only difference between the two women was hairstyle, dress and a multitude of friendly crinkles now showing around Clara's mouth and eyes. The proud look that shone in the eyes of the woman in the photo had mellowed to a calm, self-confident expression that broke into a twinkle when she looked up and saw Chloe had awakened.

"It's best not to try to fly until you've sprouted wings, my dear," she said to Chloe.

Confused, Chloe looked back silently at the little woman.

Clara moved over to the chaise. "It appears that you are fond of heights," She chirped. "You must get a very nice view of the world from the top of the garage. Perhaps you should find a less painful way down."

Chloe nodded, remembering where she had been and knowing there was no point in pretending otherwise.

"Would you like some hot tea, Chloe?" Clara suggested.

Chloe couldn't ever remember ever having had hot tea. Somehow it seemed like a good time to start. "Yes, she nodded silently and a bit uncomfortably. "Please," she answered trying to muster some semblance of etiquette.

Clara disappeared down a dim hallway leaving Chloe to examine her surroundings. From her impromptu bed in the corner on the chaise see could view the entire room without moving. It was about three times the size of Chloe's bedroom. The ceiling seemed unusually high and what Chloe had first noticed when she opened her eyes was the trim all along the wall near the ceiling. It was some kind of swirling white relief that flowed all around the room. It swirled a lot more before her eyes had fully focused. A series of three windows curved around a well-cushioned bay window seat to her right. For a moment Chloe pictured herself curled comfortably on the cushions reading a book.

Near the window seat a carved wooden pedestal supported a round, crystal vase of more peonies, pink this time, joined by columbine, iris and foxglove. Chloe could see out the window to an expanse of rich green lawn dotted with clumps of still more peonies apparently from whence these had come. Little vases of small blue flowers dotted the room on shelves, desks, and windowsills. Their fragrance was inescapable. Chloe found all the flowers more funereal than cheerful. She had had some experience in that area recently and wasn't thrilled to be reminded of it.

Dark wooden bookshelves framed the doorway through which Clara had exited. Chloe visualized a disheveled raven fluttering frantically around in the corner vainly searching for a perch. "Nevermore", he muttered repeatedly.

"Where is a bust of Pallas when you need one," she asked herself. Her head hurt.

Clara returned with the tea and a cold compress.

"The doctor's been here and gone," Clara explained. "He says you have a small concussion. You'll be fine. You need to lie still for a few days."

Chloe had no desire to move. It wasn't just her head that hurt, every part of her ached.

"You live next door to me," Chloe finally ventured after the tea began to take effect. She recognized Mrs. Fitz but had never spoken to her let alone been invited into her home.

"Yes," Clara chuckled. "I should have asked you in before. Perhaps you wouldn't have had to take such drastic measures to get here." Clara was clearly pleased with her little jokes. She paused while she examined Chloe's growing bump.

Sobering a little she continued. "That was a bad fall. I tried to call your mother but apparently she's out. I had Jack leave a note on your door so she'll come here when she gets back. That was about 6 o'clock. It's almost 8:00 now."

"She's gone to dinner and a movie with Dennis," Chloe informed her. "She'll probably be late. Sometimes I'm asleep before she gets home."

"'I'm always asleep when she gets home'" thought Chloe to herself, judiciously inclined to keep her mother's activities her own little secret.

"Well then, you'll just have to spend the night where you are," said Clara, secretly delighted to accommodate her young guest. "I'll send another note. She drew the curtains and pulled down a jigsaw puzzle.

"Flowers," thought Chloe. "What a surprise."

The effect of the puzzle was almost immediate. Chloe slept deeply, wandering through poppy fields broken into floating puzzle pieces on her way to Oz. Now and then a friendly Munchkin appeared and offered her tea.

∞

The neon sign said "Mot¬l" and boasted an "A¬A membership. The later appeared to have lost its relevancy considering the way the cars were strewn all over the parking lot. Apparently the "Mot¬l" guests had fallen off the wagon. Other indications that this might be the case were the complete lack of ice in any ice machine on the premises and the intermittent visits by local law enforcement agents in response to numerous complaints from the apartments next door regarding infractions of the noise ordinances.

Gloria, alias Mrs. Dennis, waited in the car under the flashing green vacancy sign while Mr. Dennis signed the registry and acquired a key. It wasn't exactly the evening she had been promised but she intended to make the best of it. She didn't know how to sew or to use the electron microscope but she was extraordinarily gifted in other areas. She looked forward more to a feeling of accomplishment than of physical satisfaction.

The vacancy sign was instantly negated by a hot pink neon "no" when Dennis arrived. He pushed open the glass door, identified in bold letters saying "Entrance" at eye level. The night auditor had painted the word on it himself not so much as a guide to the registration desk as to prevent the influx of weekend guests from walking into the glass, which inevitably happened more frequently as the night progressed.

Balancing four sodas under his right arm and a brown paper bag under his left, (the office was conveniently linked to a liquor store), Dennis did his best swagger across the parking lot toward Gloria. He could be charming enough when he felt like it, thought Gloria, and he wasn't unattractive, but "suave" was never an adjective that popped up when she thought of him. "Ludicrous" came briefly to mind as she watched him but she tried to dismiss it as quickly as possible. Thoughts like that would not make her task any easier.

Gloria waved her most coquettish wave. The word ludicrous crept back into her consciousness and her coquettish wave drifted into something reminiscent of Queen Elizabeth addressing her subjects as she paraded through London.

She lowered her hand and slipped it into her purse. Gloria always carried two condoms and a pair of black net stockings in the bottom of it. She felt around to make sure they were accessible. When given adequate notice she also added whatever props and toys she thought might make the evening more interesting. She was good with costumes and props. In another life the theater would have welcomed her.

As it was her bag of tricks was relatively bare, she had been expecting to dine at Maurice's followed by the late show at Le Cabaret but Dennis had decided to make it a short evening and get home to his wife. If something was going to get cut from the agenda it was inevitably the dinner and show, not the bedroom entertainment.

Dennis had never, of course, referred in any way to his phantom spouse, but Gloria fully expected she was demanding equal time. Sometimes Gloria counted on it. It gave her a refreshing break, time to restore her perspective.

In the beginning Dennis had been a strictly Holiday Inn and Radisson kind of guy. Before long he had slipped into the Best Western category. Recently he had fallen to the Road House and Bates Motel level and Gloria wasn't at all happy with the decline.

She took the keys from Dennis' pocket and unlocked the door. He hooked one arm around her and jovially hustled her inside. Drawing heavily on past experiences Gloria tried to visualize room service, a king-sized bed and a mint on the pillow. It was a difficult illusion to uphold considering the actual décor.

Once inside Dennis continued the conversation where it had left off in the car.

"I...I...I...Me...Me."

Occasionally Gloria interjected a supportive statement or joined in the conversation long enough to ask him how he knew so much about himself and all those things he was interested in. He interpreted this as encouragement and raced even more enthusiastically toward the peak of his stupendiferousness. Somehow, he never reached it. There was always more ground to cover.

Dennis had a pathological love of conversation but never wanted to risk feeling uncomfortable, even for a second. If he wasn't totally familiar with the subject, which meant it was not about him or anything directly related to him, he responded with an inaudible mumble followed by an uncomfortable silence after which a bell apparently went off in his head signaling the start of another race to the Summit of Dennis. The unfamiliar topic, possible anything whatsoever to do with Gloria, was summarily dismissed as if it had been exhausted by hours of discussion, or had not existed at all.

Essentially Dennis was incapable of thought. His conversations were based on the most basic tenets of behavioral science, i.e., if A is said then it is countered with B; B elicits C and only C; D is inevitably followed by E, if Dennis could focus his attention that long. It all progressed in a very predictable sequence. Most of the input never even went to his brain but got as far as his spinal cord and was routed back to his mouth via reflex action, no thought necessary. He did this so rapidly that it almost appeared as if he were cognizant.

Dennis hated thought. Made him uncomfortable. Made him sweat.

In order for Gloria to buy into such a conversation she had to be willing to feed him the A for his B or the B for his C and so forth. It wasn't a difficult job and was somewhat rewarding in a sort of Zen sense, requiring transcendence of her own ego as it did. It could be very relaxing. After a while her own thought processes slowed to a standstill and when she was dropped off at home her mind often felt refreshed and wide awake, as if she had been in a deep sleep for hours. This was not always welcome at one or two in the morning.

Bit by bit Gloria lost all depth of personality. After only a few short weeks the Gloria that Dennis knew was about one micron thick. He could have slid her between the pages of a book if he ever bothered to pick one up. That's the way he liked her. That's the way he groomed and cultivated her. Like a great sculptor he whittled away everything about Gloria that didn't reflect him and only him and he sincerely admired what he had wrought. Fortunately, Gloria saved all the little discarded pieces in a shoe box in the back of her closet. Occasionally she took them out and scattered them across her bed as a reminder of who she had been. She planned to reconstruct herself someday, but the blueprints were getting harder and harder to remember.

Dennis flipped on the TV. and tossed down his first rum and coke while Gloria went into the bathroom to enhance her mystique with fishnet. When she returned Dennis was reclining on the bed, second cocktail in hand, spouting Dennisisms by the score.

"Gloria, if I've said it once I've said it a million times…. If it was up to me….I could have told them…."

Gloria leaned back on the desk and sipped her rum slowly, nodding intermittently as the alcohol took effect.

The subject turned to cars, he liked hers. She liked his.

Eventually he dropped his boxers and she admired his shiny red engine.

He was crazy about her sleek, ample fenders.

"Baby, baby, baby," he said.

"Oooh, ooh, ooh," she said.

It was the most meaningful conversation they had had all night.

9
CLARA

Chloe awoke a second time to the smell of tea and toast. Clara brought it on a tray with two soft boiled eggs and a glass of orange juice on the side. It had been some time since Clara had had anyone to pamper, and she was taking full advantage of the opportunity.

Despite the possibility of a warm breakfast, Chloe wasn't entirely delighted to awaken in a strange place. She had the impulse to bolt. She wondered where her clothes were. If she had been more awake her eyes would have darted around the room searching for them. As it was her eyes failed to respond to the darting command, but her nose responded well to the food. Chloe relaxed and accepted her fate.

She and Clara exchanged "good mornings" and Clara opened the curtains. It was raining again. This time it was not so magical, it was just plain gloomy.

Clara brought in a second tray for herself and she and Chloe watched the storm worsen as they ate. Clara asked about Chloe's school and Chloe responded politely. Chloe asked about Clara's flowers and Clara responded more cheerfully. Still, the morning wasn't going very well and both Chloe and Clara wished for some word from Chloe's mother.

Clara set down her tea and asked Chloe if she felt up to a tour of the house. Chloe's acceptance was the most enthusiastic response Clara had elicited since the child's arrival.

With relief Chloe spread her arms wide as Clara slipped her into a Japanese robe elaborately embroidered with bats and peonies. Clara artfully scooped the dragging gown off the floor and tied it up to a more reasonable length. The silk billowed over the sash and the sleeves slid down to Chloe's fingertips. Chloe's skin responded with curiosity to silk when it had expected flannel, a more fitting material in her mind for an old woman cloistered (she had been precociously reading Hamlet and had become fond of the word cloistered) alone in a big, dusty, old house. She declined the offer of the peculiar looking white stocking-slippers with the split toes and obediently followed Mrs. Fitz barefooted under the imaginary raven, past the non-existent bust of Pallus, through the dark doorway and out of the sitting room.

The big, dusty, old house, as Chloe had judged it from the outside, though bigger even than expected, was not at all dusty or ill kept in any way. The neglected facade the three-story Victorian showed to the outside world housed an elegant and precisely arranged interior flawed only by the slightly stale odor old houses acquire when children's voices fade and family dinners no longer exist.

They passed through the nearly empty dining room and across the hard, cold, stone floor of the front entryway. Chloe tried to pay attention to Clara's narrative but Clara's text could not compete with the illustrations. The moment she reached for the swooping, black banister and began ascending the staircase, Chloe was lost in the very softness of the carpet under her feet. She missed the tale's introduction which started not with "when I was a child..." but with "once upon a time...". Preoccupied with the elaborately carved stairway and the figures dancing about under the willows in the wallpaper, Chloe vaguely heard "in a nearby kingdom lived a handsome prince." At the top of the stairs Chloe was almost left behind as she paused to gaze off the landing and down to the polished flagged stones below, where the cut glass windows in the great front door sparkled with every flash of lightning.

Clara was halfway down the first hallway oblivious to her absence before Chloe ran to catch up. They were reunited just in time to enter the first bedroom.

Chloe didn't need to hear the passage introducing the princes, the evidence was clearly displayed before her. Clara, however, would never carry the fairy tale analogy that far. Although in her heart her children were royalty, calling her sons princes would have implied a degree of spoiling and vanity which Clara was not capable of by virtue of her character or of her finances. Clara justified the trappings of her boy's room as educational enhancement, a creative environment. Chloe saw a palatial playground.

Henry, Alexander and their father had built the train set to circle the room and traverse the walls. Clara and Alexander had made the extravagant tiger kite that hung from the ceiling, its tail trailing back and forth towards the corner. Henry collected the wind-up toys on the shelf: the monkey that played the drum, the dog that did somersaults, the two clowns that played catch, and others. His father had taught him to take them apart and put them back together perfectly. By the time he was nine he could reconstruct each of them with no help whatsoever. Alexander had the ant farm, now void of ants. His first fishing pole was mounted on the wall with a picture of the whole family at the lake. It was this picture of everyone in their bathing suits, knee deep in water and drowning in sunshine that made Chloe turn abruptly and leave the room.

"What's in those rooms?" she asked Mrs. Fitz, pointing down the hall.

She wanted to run down the hall, away from the boy's room, the room that reminded her of everything her life had never been.

Clara sensed Chloe's distress and strode down the hallway. For a woman five foot four she strode surprisingly well.

"Chloe, are you coming?" asked Clara, looking back.

Thunder rolled. The windows rattled. Chloe ran to catch up.

"When each of my sons turned ten they moved into these rooms," Clara explained, pointing to the pair of doorways Chloe had indicated. They kept these rooms until they went off to college.

Chloe stepped into the room on the right. Although Clara was still talking, Chloe stopped listening altogether the moment she passed through the doorway.

"I would never leave this room," Chloe immediately thought to herself.

Next to the window, which stretched almost from floor to ceiling, as they commonly do in very old houses, was Henry's bed. It was a bed like Chloe had never seen before. The polished, dark wood frame was alive with flora and fauna never before seen in any of the books Chloe had ever visited. There was a tall post at each corner shaped with clawed feet at the bottom and a hawk-like head at the top. The posts were smooth and rounded inviting her to run her hand over the warm contours. Atop the tall, sleek, nearly black head board a giant bird spread its wings, protecting whoever slumbered beneath from unknown creatures of the night. Its deep angular eyes scanned the room searching for intruders. The posts at the foot of the bed morphed at their peaks into lesser birds of prey positioned to respond to the command of their master.

Chloe looked up at Clara.

"May I?" she asked.

"Of course," replied Clara, who had terminated her diatribe of her son's scholastic achievements and was quietly and quizzically watching Chloe.

Chloe turned and pulled herself up onto the edge of the bed, curling her bare toes over the portion of the wooden frame that ran vertically between the posts. From here she looked around the room.

There was a desk in the corner with pen and pencil laid impeccably to the right, paper in the middle and a lamp with a metal stand and frosted shade to the left. The shelf above held a dictionary, thesaurus, and atlas. The accompanying chair was equally formal with a straight, wooden back and hard, wooden seat holding just a hint of a cushion. This was a chair designed to keep its occupant alert and focused on whatever technical or creative task that was put before him.

"I would sit in that chair for hours," Chloe whispered.

One entire bedroom wall was covered with book shelves. Chloe slipped off the bed and went to read the titles.

"Where is Henry now?" asked Chloe as she studied the shelves. Secretly she hoped somehow that he lived just down the street and needed a little girl to call his own.

Boston," replied Clara, a little sadly. He moved there after he came home from the war. Now he's married and has a daughter about your age. He's a lawyer, she added with pride.

Chloe tried to hide her disappointment. That was pretty far away. Not exactly the other side of the block. Besides, what would he do with two daughters her age?

"They visit a couple times every year," Clara added, trying to sound more positive.

"What's in the other room?" Chloe asked as she walked out the door. She was not one to dwell on disappointment.

Alexander's room was amazing in its own right. The model airplanes that hung from thin wires to the ceiling had never seen the inside of a box. They shared the air space with motorized birds decked in colorful plumage and planets revolving forever around the sun.

The bookshelves supported as many mineral specimens as they did books. Great crystals hanging from the windows shattered the light sprinkling rainbows across the floor. A microscope sat on the desk. Hockey sticks were parked in the corner.

Chloe correctly identified the Cecropia moth mounted above the bed, a more moderate version of his brother's. Made of the same deep hued wood, this bed, although beautifully carved with swooping curves and graceful posts, lacked phantasmagoric creatures. Alexander had enough creatures and paraphernalia sharing his room without incorporating them in the furniture.

Chloe thought it all very impressive but was ready to move on. Now that she had tasted tea she knew this was not her cup. Clara followed her down the corridor pointing out her own room as they passed by. The two glanced in without stopping. Chloe caught a glimpse of unfamiliar maps on the wall and Japanese prints over the bed. Her curiosity was peaked but Clara hurried her along with something else in mind. They reached the end of the hall where Chloe began to descend the back stairs, an invention she was unfamiliar with but found intriguing. She felt like running down the back stairs and up the front over and over again, (the pain killers had kicked in). Clara stopped her and reached for the stout cord that hung from the ceiling.

Clara pulled the cord with both of her small but strong little arms and down came a compact wooden stairway leading to the attic. Chloe ascended first with Clara close behind, to prevent another fall. How would she explain that to Chloe's mother?

As Chloe's head disappeared from the second-floor hallway it appeared, as if by magic, in the room above. This attic was apparently visited as often as the hayloft of the garage had been, however it was bigger and contained even more cast-off junk lurking about in the haze. Chloe really had no desire to explore this place and for a moment wondered what she was doing here in a strange old house with a clearly peculiar old lady in her dark and ominous attic. Had she really seen any note sent off to her mother? Did anyone actually know where she was? Her heart began to beat faster and she tried to back down the ladder, attempting to decline this invitation after all.

Clara urged her on, assuring her that what was in store was right up her alley. Chloe doubted it but surmised that if Mrs. Fitz was planning to do her in she could have done it many times over by now and saved herself the trouble of making breakfast.

Chloe climbed through the hole in the ceiling and dusted herself off as Clara rose to her side. Without pausing Clara continued briskly across the room, dodging box to the left and box to the right and low, long trunks between until she reached another ladder leading to another hole in the ceiling. Chloe was beginning to feel like Alice falling down the rabbit hole in reverse and had given up any thought of gaining control of the situation.

This time Chloe followed Clara upward, pausing only for her guide to lift the heavy lid at the top of the ladder before the two rose into the wind and the weather and onto the roof. Chloe inhaled sharply as the chilly air struck her face. She was stunned. The whole of Chicago was at her cold little bare feet. She could even see the lake, at least she believed she could see the lake. Clara was right; this really was right up her alley.

The better part of the storm had passing and the lightning could only be seen far off in the direction of the lake. Echoes of thunder reverberated long after the lightening could be seen. The clouds above her were breaking up, the dark grays and blacks were becoming edged with cream and yellow, then finally blue. Rays of sunshine streaked across the sky. Chloe and Clara stood together on the widow's walk and watched the sun sweep over the city.

Moments later Gloria let the backdoor slam and set a direct path for the Fitz' house. Clara saw her cross the yard and fumble through the opening in the pea shrubs. As Gloria approached the backdoor Clara called and waved from above.

"We'll be right down," Clara shouted, gleeful at the prospect of yet another visitor. "Go right in."

The call that drifted down to Gloria was barely audible. When it finally registered she had difficulty pinpointing its origin. She looked around, slightly annoyed by her own confusion. Another faint call dropped out of the sky. She looked up and saw an elderly woman precariously waving her inside from the roof top. She waved back and disappeared into the house, vaguely wondering what the old bird was doing up there.

Chloe paid no attention. She stood on the widow's walk, mesmerized by the horizon, closer to the sky than she had ever been before. She was not distracted by the activity below; it was the glimpse of Beyond that held her attention.

Clara interrupted Chloe's reverie and led her back down the rabbit hole to the sitting room where her mother waited, a little uncomfortably, with patience born solely from determination. It had been late the night before when Gloria discovered the note on her door. She had assumed Chloe was all right or they would have sent her to the hospital. She went to bed unconcerned and slept late, later than she had intended. Now her façade of patience and concern was fragile and covered a soft, spongy interior that longed for coffee and an hour or so of privacy to firm it up.

Gloria looked at Chloe, a wisp of a child lost in the bunched-up dressing gown.

With unexpected concern, Gloria asked, "Chloe Honey, how's your head?"

The question seemed normal enough to Clara but surprised both Gloria and Chloe with its spontaneity and sincerity.

Chloe was too stunned to speak so she turned her head to reveal to her mother the lump on her temple that was becoming increasingly colorful as the hours passed.

"Jesus Christ, Chloe," her mother blurted out. "That must hurt like hell."

Chloe's eyes widened and flashed at her mother.

"Excuse me but that's a nasty bump. I wasn't expecting anything like that." Gloria continued, modifying her choice of words.

She raised an eyebrow and flashed Chloe an expression that read, "Better?"

It was a level of rapport mother and daughter had never before achieved. They were both secretly pleased with their accomplishment.

Clara was not at all offended. Gloria was the shocked and concerned mother. Chloe was saved from embarrassment.

After a brief discussion regarding the doctor's orders, Chloe and Gloria left together savoring a warm glow of mutual understanding that lasted all the way to their own back door. Once inside Gloria handed Chloe the bottle of codeine and told her to go to bed and take one when it hurt. Then she made coffee. She considered pouring a cup or two directly over her head but rejected the idea in favor of inhaling it instead. She no longer day dreamed and pondered the meaning of her life. Her tawdry little affair with Dennis provided a multitude of petty problems to dwell on. They conveniently displaced any questions of universal proportions. Metaphysical issues had become passé.

Her thoughts, limited though they were, were suddenly interrupted by a maternal feeling of concern for Chloe's well-being. She wasn't entirely sure what to do with it. She decided to ask Chloe, Chloe would know. She poured another cup of coffee and headed up to Chloe's room.

Chloe was asleep. Gloria looked around the room, a stranger to her daughter's life.

"She always has been sort of a boring child," Gloria thought as she saw row upon row of books on Chloe's shelves, each book arranged meticulously in alphabetical order.

"Compulsive little thing." She added, when she saw Chloe's clothes carefully hung according to category, length, and color in her closet.

"I wonder what she does for fun."

Gloria walked over to the desk by the window where Chloe's paper and drawing pencils were neatly set to the side. She looked down to the backyard where Chloe's bike leaned against a tree.

"I guess she's OK then," she told herself.

She turned and picked up the bottle of codeine on the table next to the bed. After reading it she tucked it in her pocket and looked down at Chloe. She brushed the hair from Chloe's cheek and left the room.

10
REFUGE

It was impossible to say exactly when Chloe awoke the next morning. She was at Clara's backdoor by 8:00. She wanted to go earlier but thought it might be impolite to arrive before breakfast. Clara, an early riser herself, opened the screen door with tea and toast in hand. She had already been out to weed the tomatoes and was just taking a break before returning to fertilize a few perennials. She was about to offer Chloe a bite to eat but recognized immediately that food was not what Chloe was looking for.

She tipped her head forward, looked over the top of her reading glasses, and said simply, "Come down when you get hungry. I'll make you something."

Chloe was half way up the stairs before Clara added, "And be careful. Stay inside the railing."

Chloe was gone in a flash.

Clara wasn't a woman who would have enjoyed just any child around the house. She was fortunate that Chloe was the one that had dropped into her garden. She liked Chloe's point of view, albeit a little bizarre. The more Clara got to know her (and her mother) the more grateful she became that Chloe was not yet a homicidal maniac nor intensely self-destructive. With a little kindness all that could be averted, she told herself. Clara was up to it. She liked a good challenge.

It wasn't until her third visit to the widow's walk that Chloe appeared at the threshold of the kitchen. Clara knew Chloe would come around eventually. Like trying to tempt a feral kitten onto the back porch with a bowl of milk, Clara had waited patiently, holding out company and kindness for the taking.

"Mrs. Fitz?" Chloe said quietly from the doorway to the sitting room.

Clara looked up warmly, but with enough reserve not to frighten off this strange little creature.

"I'm kind of hungry," Chloe ventured cautiously.

Clara recognized her cue.

"What did you have in mind?" Clara asked.

"I don't know. What have you got," responded Chloe.

"Come into the kitchen. Let's see what we can find."

The raven above the doorway craned his neck to watch Chloe pass beneath him. Chloe tried to ignore him.

The kitchen was stocked with sugar cookies, milk, carrots, apple juice, and peanut butter. For those cooler days Clara had bought hot chocolate and chicken noodle soup. A jar of red licorice and M&M's sat on the end of the counter. There was enough tea to support another Boston uprising. Clara loved a good project.

Once in the kitchen Chloe climbed up onto the wooden stool near the sink. Clara opened her cupboards wide for Chloe to see. Naturally Chloe immediately looked past everything Clara had stocked for her and honed directly in onto a can of tuna in the back.

"Tuna sandwich it is then," said Clara. She made a mental note to buy more tuna.

A comfortable silence filled the room while Clara made the sandwich and Chloe watched. Both Clara and Chloe were used to silence. It didn't bother either of them.

When Clara put the sandwich on the kitchen table Chloe slid off the stool and sat across from Clara and her fresh cup of tea. Chloe ate half of her sandwich before Clara attempted conversation.

"So Chloe," ventured Clara, "now that you've tried it out a few times what do you think of my widow's walk?"

Clara stirred her tea.

Chloe searched for an adequate response. She had never talked much and it was hard for her to explain about Beyond. After a short pause during which she studied Clara's face intently she could only come up with, "I like it very much, Mrs. Fitz. I like it just fine."

Gaining some confidence at having successfully entered into the conversation, Chloe paused and then added, "Do you go up there very much?"

"I shouldn't have said that," she thought immediately. "That's none of my business. She won't let me come back."

"I used to go up every day in the summers," said Clara, pleased that Chloe had asked her. Clara was a story teller at heart and it warmed her inside to reminisce.

"I'd stand at the railing and watch for my husband as he came home from work every day. We would wave to each other and then I'd run down as fast as I could to meet him at the front door. When the boys were born I'd try to give them a late nap so I could go up without worrying about them. I got out of the habit when they refused to sleep in the afternoon.

"You know there aren't many widow's walks around here," she added. "They're a seacoast invention. Women would stand up there and watch for ships to return home carrying their husbands, fathers, and sons. Charles had it built just for fun. He always dreamed of living on the coast. We used to sit together up there drinking ice tea in the summer, watching the trains come and go in the distance.

She paused.

"I think you would have liked him, Chloe," she said with conviction.

She smiled warmly and added resolutely. "I know he would have liked you."

Chloe was at a loss as to what to say next. This time she was a little uncomfortable with the silence.

"Do you suppose next time I could have an orange soda?" she blurted out.

Her heart went to her throat.

"That was really stupid," she told herself.

Clara laughed. It was a nice laugh.

"I'll have to write it down. I can't remember anything these days."

She reached for the paper and pencil that lay near the window and began a grocery list.

"What else was I going to get her?" she wondered. "There was something else."

But it had escaped her.

I've got an appointment, Chloe, I've got to go out," Clara said when Chloe had finished her sandwich. "You run on home now. I'll see you later."

Obediently, Chloe got up to leave.

"Thank you for the lunch, Mrs. Fitz." She said politely. "I enjoyed it very much."

Then she disappeared out the back door.

Clara watched through the window as Chloe crossed the yard toward the pea shrubs. She was about to pass through when she stopped, turned and walked into the center of the asparagus patch. She put her arms straight out from her sides and spun, laughing as the tall fronds tickled her bare arms.

11
DAY CAMP

That was the beginning of the happiest summer Chloe could remember. The trauma of earlier weeks was banished to the recesses of her mind along with the collection of ill-gotten parenting skills that were no longer required of her.

Gloria took a job as a receptionist and was learning to type. The activity made her insanely frustrated but as long as she appeared to be trying her boss retained her as an attractive addition to the interior design of his arty front office. Her voice was pleasant, her demeanor was subservient, and her skirt was short. His clients no longer objected to spending long periods of time in her presence as he dallied in his private office with a variety of lady friends or female employees who naively expected a promotion, a raise, or a weekend at his non-existent summer home on the white sand beaches of some fairy tale lake in northern Michigan.

The pay was even more insulting than the environment but Gloria overlooked both. She took the position more as a means to fill her time than her pocketbook. She liked to think of the position as a pastime rather than a job. That way she could convince herself she had not lowered her no bars, no education, no job standards. It wasn't far from the truth. The stipend she brought home would never have supported the two of them but it did help slow the steady flow of funds from her porous bank account.

She fulfilled her parental obligations by enrolling Chloe in one of those summer day camps that walked children through the forest preserves in hideously high temperatures stopping only for water and peanut butter sandwiches. By the time they were returned to their parents each day heat exhaustion and clogged bowels prevented them from mustering the strength to complain. Parents jumped on the chance to interpret this as "all tired out from having a good time" and sent them back day after day.

Chloe had the good sense and transportation savvy to hail a taxi home each day as soon as her mother sped off in the other direction. She financed this maneuver with a small savings she had tucked away when she had led her mother around by the hand instructing her to sign checks to get the two of them through each day. At that time, she had been none too sure of her mother's potential for recovery and decided it was important to keep a handle on the New South Wales Fund which she kept in an envelope taped to the top of the inside of her desk drawer. The funds for reaching New South Wales were now evaporating rapidly. Fortunately, the need to escape was diminishing at an equal rate. Chloe was content simply to pass through the opening in the hedge and into the care of Mrs. Fitz.

Monday through Friday throughout the month of July and well into August Chloe was welcomed into the garden with a genteel breakfast of tea, toast and a soft-boiled egg garnished neatly with fresh fruit and a sprig of mint. Mrs. Fitz did so enjoy a refined breakfast and a way to justify the existence of her unruly mint patch. Chloe's tea, of course, was mostly milk; Clara saw to that. She and Chloe sat at a small cast iron table near the roses and practiced the fine art of conversation, a skill Chloe had never learned and Clara had not used in a long time.

Initially, Clara did most of the talking. She introduced Chloe to the garden and taught her the individual needs of each plant that Chloe helped her tend. If Chloe became restless, as children naturally do, Clara sent her off on her bicycle to circle the neighborhood a few times before lunch. Clara never asked where Gloria was or where Chloe was expected to be. She firmly believed that if you don't want to know the answer, don't ask the question.

Chloe was a fast learner. By the end of the first week she proved to be both an excellent horticulturist and a budding conversationalist. She was Clara's hands when it came to pinching the spent flowers from the tall campanulas and tangled columbine. She had a gentle touch when it came to coaxing apart the roots of crowded seedlings. She had an eye for color when she chose blooms for the sitting room table. All these she did to make herself useful, hopefully indispensable, to Mrs. Fitz. To be sure, Chloe liked the garden, but what she really loved was Clara.

Once Clara had broken the ice with the horticultural classes the two cautiously moved on to other subjects. They pretty much avoided anecdotes regarding their friends, Chloe had never made any and most of Clara's were dead. This could have put a real damper on the conversation but the void was filled primarily with fictional characters and their creators. Chloe brought up a mutual acquaintance, Mr. E. Poe, and they "oohed" and "aahed" together at the terrible fates of his creations; pits, pendulums, beating hearts and the like. Off to a good start, they began to enlarge their circle of friends. Chloe had never met Lenore but Clara assured her that she would find her lost on the shelves of her sitting room. Chloe ran into the house to find her.

Clara, like so many other women brought up in the Victorian era, was particularly fond of Tennyson and Kipling. Now their poems flooded back to her and she retold them with vigor. Tennyson was next. Chloe loved the rhythm of the Tennyson's six hundred men riding heroically into the Valley of Death. So tragic. So heart wrenching. So wonderfully rhythmic.

Clara sent Chloe into the house one more time to retrieve the Kipling volume from the shelf. For the rest of that week they submerged themselves in the tale of Mohamed Khan, son of the Ressaldar, the Colonel, and the heroic Kammel until Chloe knew it by heart.

"There is neither East nor West, border nor breed nor birth," Chloe recited proudly as she stood in front of a tall frond of elephant fern before her rapt audience. Chloe liked the way the "Bs" burst from her mouth in quick succession. She continued flawlessly to the very end as brave men galloped here and there, breech bolts snicking every which way. "Though they come from the ends of the earth!" she finished exultantly and out of breath.

Clara applauded vigorously. Chloe curtsied, then bowed, then took her seat at the little table. They both laughed in the sunshine. Clara sipped a little more tea and Chloe sucked on another orange slice before hopping on her over-sized, second hand Schwinn and taking a long spin around the block.

After lunch Chloe habitually took a book to the widow's walk and lay on a towel in the sun. It might have been all the stretching out across the terrycloth that encouraged her legs to grow two inches that summer. Maybe it was the sunshine that helped calm her nerves and made her teeth gleam when her newly discovered grin spread across her beautifully tanned face. Maybe her good looks were an inevitable part of continually growing into her role as Gloria's daughter. Whatever it was, nature or nurture, Chloe passed her tenth birthday, August 20, 1959, with all the indications that she would be what is traditionally referred to as an early bloomer.

Although Clara noticed the changes, Chloe herself, who had no use for mirrors, was oblivious to them. Chloe hadn't noticed her shorts becoming shorter or her summer tops becoming scantier. She lay on her stomach on the widow's walk with her legs waving innocently in the air like slender stalks of wheat blowing in the afternoon breeze. The sun glistened off the sparkling blonde down on her graceful limbs. Her back was arched in a lazy crescent, her weight resting on her elbows as she read.

She lay down her book and flipped onto her back. The tails of her sleeveless blouse were tied up in a knot to reveal a long expanse of lean 10-year-old midriff stretching toward the narrow waistband of her crisp white shorts. The heat of the afternoon coaxed tiny droplets of perspiration to the surface of Chloe's baby soft skin. They journeyed slowly around each delicate, sun bleached hair and rolled erratically across her belly before dripping off her sides onto her towel.

Her lids fell shut to protect her tired eyes from the merciless mid-August sun. For a short-time Chloe gave in to the sensation that all the atoms of her being were being drawn down into a large puddle beneath her and melting into the hard surface of the roof. She tried to regain enough control of her mind to imagine the handsome Colonel racing feverishly across the desert in pursuit of the elusive and equally attractive Kamel, but they kept getting lost in the storm of hot swirling jinns that the sun was projecting through her delicate eyelids. Oranges and reds spun through a world of yellow and black. Her breath came short and shallow. When she barely had the strength left to draw one more, she reached for her bottle of water and poured it over her face and stomach.

She sat up and opened her eyes.

"Too hot!" she gasped.

She rolled her book and bottle tightly in her towel and dropped them through the roof into the attic. She crawled down after them and pulled the lid tightly over her head.

∞

Gloria, too was gasping in the heat. She was sticky and uncomfortable and had nothing nice to say about Chicago in the summer. Her boss refused to give her an air conditioning unit although the one in his office was so effective she could feel the cool breeze roll out every time he opened his door. She considered getting back at him by wearing long skirts and high collared dresses until his clients, robbed of the source of their delight, lost all patience with him. She tried it one day and he clearly looked angry and harassed by mid-afternoon. She, however, was on the brink of heat stroke. The clever plan was discontinued.

For the remainder of the week she wore as little as possible. She sat with a bowl of ice cubes on her desk and ran one slowly across her forehead, then back across her chest, whenever she got the chance. The performance did not result in the installation of an air conditioning unit but it did provide Gloria with its own brand of entertainment. After chilling her chest, she liked to hold the cube with the tips of her blood red fingernails and suck on it until it dissolved. She had seen this done in a movie once and the effect had been very amusing. She feigned reading a book throughout the exhibition but peaked over the top intermittently to see how her audience was responding. The reviews were mixed. Women aghast tried in vain not to watch while men tripped over each other to get her another bowl of ice every time she ran out.

This little exhibition went on for two or three days before Gloria tired of it. When both the heat and the humidity continued to hang in the high nineties for three consecutive afternoons Gloria announced that she was going home sick and slammed the door behind her.

If she had expected some relief outside the office Gloria was sorely disappointed. Temperatures soared. There was no escape.

Automobile fumes refused to dissipate and hung on every drop of moisture. Tempers flared like sunspots wherever she went. Gloria edged her way across town as horns blared around her and tires screeched like banshees.

She passed the park where she had dropped Chloe off that morning and suddenly decided to double back and pick her up early. She swung an illegal U-turn at the end of the block and pulled up at Camp Central.

In a juvenile version of Hieronymus Bosch meets Salvador Dali, dehydrated children were draped everywhere across park benches and picnic tables. Others thrashed the kids in front of them with sticks for first rights at the water fountain. Craft tables were overturned and abandoned in favor of mud fights on the river bank. Those that couldn't make it to the water sat dejectedly on the ground, strings of shells and feathers dangling from their necks or abandoned in the grass nearby. Counselors halfheartedly shouted at their wards to stay out of the water. Others, who had accepted that their lack of control would inevitably cost them their jobs, cast all responsibility to the winds and sat waist deep in the water themselves. Occasionally one of these would call out to an older kid to snag one of the younger ones who was drifting dangerously downstream.

Gloria wasn't particularly appalled by the sight, she just wanted to find Chloe and get out as fast as possible. She called to a pair of the counselors seated in the river.

"Hello," she shouted from the river bank. "Hello. Would one of you find you find my daughter for me? Her name is Chloe. I want to take her home."

No response.

"Excuse me," she shouted a little more aggressively. "You two in the water. Counselors. Where's Chloe. I want to go home."

No response. The counselors sat mutely staring at the currents.

Gloria took off her shoes and waded into the water, slipping precariously on the mud and rocks.

"Listen you two. I want you to find my kid so I can get out of here."

The girl on the left looked up at Gloria.

"What's her name?" she asked none too enthusiastically.

"Chloe. She's ten. Brown hair. Shoulder length. Quiet kid. Green eyes. High cheek bones. Kind of skinny."

"No, skinny, brown haired ten-year old girls here," the boy next to her snorted sarcastically.

"Really," the girl said, trying to be a little more helpful now. "There really isn't a Chloe here. There's fifty kids and I collect all the role sheets every day and read them before I hand them in. We've never had a Chloe."

"Sarah," the boy shouted to a little girl in the river. "Grab Harry. He's gone under again over by that big rock. There's a hole there. Reach in and pull him out."

"That kid's got no sense," he mumbled to himself. "Deserves to drown."

"She has to be here, Gloria sputtered impatiently beginning to suspect some kind of gross incompetence before her. "I drop her off at that corner at 8:30 every day."

She pointed to the street behind her.

The girl counselor looked at her blankly.

The guy, his interest suddenly peaked, remembered seeing a kid getting out of a red Bel Aire every day.

"Nice car," he said. "She always takes off in a taxi."

"That couldn't be Chloe. She goes to camp every day." Gloria insisted. "I paid for it."

The counselors glanced at each other and waited patiently for Gloria to catch on.

When her right brain and her left brain finally got around to communicating with each other her mouth did not say, "Oh that little rascal." It was quite a bit more expressive.

Gloria spun around in the mud and stomped toward the safety of the bank. She would have made it, too, if it hadn't been for that one flat piece of mossy shale disguised as a foothold. Gloria slid abruptly sideways, dropped her shoes and landed on her left knee in the slime. She stumbled to her feet retrieved her irreparably damaged footwear and fumbled up the bank.

Gloria was livid. Limpid children came to life and clawed their way over each other to get out of her way. Counselors who had casually watched the near-death experiences of their wards in the water suddenly leaped up and snatched little children out of her path. All eyes were on Gloria.

Gloria tripped again when a string of beads acted like a bola around her ankles. She nearly crushed a five-year old in the process. Unremorseful, Gloria fumbled to her feet fuming. She grabbed a roll of paper towels from a picnic bench and mopped the slime from her hands and legs as she headed for the car, muddy towels flying in her wake. She flung the remainder of the roll over her shoulder and threw herself behind the wheel. She slammed the door and sped off.

A single counselor began to clap. Another joined in. Then applause rose up from the whole camp with whooping and cheering throughout.

∞

"I did not spend good money for you to sit home pouting unsupervised every day, Chloe!" Gloria shouted.

The more she shouted the more upset she got. She only had one rule for herself after the "no adult education" commandment, and that was "never scream at your kids". Ignore them but you couldn't scream at them. Gloria had had a great deal of experience being screamed at herself and always swore she would not ever be the screamer. The more she screamed the angrier she got, as much at herself and all the people who had screamed at her as with Chloe. It made her shout even louder. She began shouting at her boss and yelling at her ex. She laid into Dennis in a big way and then moved on to other wrongs that had been dealt her. She berated her psychiatrists, her third-grade teacher, and the ladies at the Episcopal Church.

There was no stopping her. She finished up by hating the color of her living room and detesting the pattern on the couch just before she fell, exhausted upon it, sweat dripping from her face and arms.

Chloe was nowhere in sight. When Gloria had stopped yelling at Chloe and turned her torrent of abuse on her father, Chloe, in the interest of self-preservation, slipped out the back. Once outside her impulse to get as far away as possible was replaced with a curiosity to hear what her mother had to say. She flattened herself against the house and slid behind the junipers until she was under the open living room window.

By the time the tirade subsided, Chloe didn't know what to think. First she decided that her mother was a very scary person. Then she wanted something to drink. She went back in the house.

She looked back to make sure the back door was open in case a hasty retreat was necessary.

"Want some ice tea?" she asked in the interest of reconciliation. She watched her mother cautiously from the kitchen doorway.

"Yes," said Gloria.

Chloe opened the frig and got an ice tea for her mother and an orange pop for herself.

"Thanks" said Gloria.

"Sure," said Chloe as she sat down.

They both sat silently for a moment considering just ignoring the past 15 minutes.

Then Chloe, with her new-found conversational skills said, "I didn't stay home pouting unsupervised. I was next door with Mrs. Fitz."

"Really?" said Gloria drolly.

Chloe told her story, an abbreviated version.

Gloria listened silently, too tired to have an opinion at this point.

"I'm, going to take a shower," she said.

That evening the temperatures dropped. Then the rain came.

12

NEVERMORE

Chloe ducked through the pea shrubs and lifted her head just as an enormous flock of cackling, grey birds dropped out of the sky and perched on the clothes lines, bushes and tomato vines of Mrs. Fitz' garden. They barely hesitated before dropping the rest of the way to the ground to gobble up the flesh and seeds of the vegetable garden decimated by rain and hail the night before. The storm had slashed the garden beyond recognition. The birds, in the throes of feasting, ignored Chloe as she waded through them on her way to the back door. Occasionally one would feign flight by jumping into the air and drifting a few feet away out of Chloe's path while the rest remained indifferent to her.

The rained had stopped an hour earlier but continued to drip from broken branches, sodden petals and glistening greenery. Clara was not in the garden.

"She can't bear to see it," Chloe thought to herself. "Even I can barely look at it."

Chloe's throat tightened and she timidly opened the back door. She called to Mrs. Fitz.

"Good morning, Chloe," Clara said brightly.

"Good morning," replied Chloe, wondering what could possibly be good about it.

She felt like crying.

"Why so glum?" asked Clara. It was a rhetorical question.

Chloe looked sadly out the window.

"The garden." Clara said, trying to hide her own disappointment. "It's not so bad. The flowers will come back next week. As for the vegetables, they're being transformed into birds. I love birds. Now I feel we've been growing birds as well as tomatoes."

She and Chloe stood together and stared silently out the window.

"I have to admit I'm not as fond of those noisy starlings," she continued, referring to the flock outside her window. "But there have been others here, too. I was up very early today, and there were some very nice tanagers, those pretty grosbeaks and a few blackbirds, the ones with the red tips on their wings. They have lovely voices."

Chloe could see that Mrs. Fitz looked tired. She suddenly wondered how old Mrs. Fitz really was.

"Chloe," said Clara. Her voice had turned gentle and serious, "Let's sit down. I want to talk to you."

Clara sat down without making a cup of tea. Chloe lowered herself cautiously into the chair across from her. Only bad news could possibly follow that introduction.

"Alexander called last night," said Clara. "He and Henry have been talking to Jack about me. Jack told them some nonsense about my memory. He thinks I'm getting forgetful," she said in a voice that sounded slightly offended, a little defensive and perhaps even worried.

"Talking about me behind my back'" she said softly, looking out the window again.

Chloe wanted to protest but couldn't prevent herself from thinking of the tea water boiling dry three times last week, the missed doctor's appointment, and the untimely breakfast.

Chloe had come down from the roof last Wednesday afternoon and was just going out the back door when Clara said, "Chloe, you're early. Help me take the breakfast tray to the garden."

She reminded Mrs. Fitz of the time and Clara countered with, "Breakfast? Did I say breakfast? I meant tea tray. Let's sit in the garden with it."

Chloe knew what was coming next.

"I'll watch out for you," she said. "I'll come every day and stay longer. I'll sleep here if you want."

"That's very kind, Chloe," said Clara. "I'm sure you would. But you will have to go back to school soon. Besides, your mother would miss you."

Chloe thought not.

Clara paused and looked out the window again.

"Apparently my sons have been discussing me for some time now. They've flipped a coin for me," she said with a hint of bitterness Chloe had never heard from her before. The tone was gone immediately and Mrs. Fitz said more cheerfully, "I'm going to live with Alexander at Muir Beach. I think California will be a nice change. Not so dreadfully cold in the winter. I wish Charles was coming, and you, too, Chloe."

She took Chloe's hand in hers and held it tightly.

"I'm sorry, Chloe." she said simply.

Then she took Chloe's face in her hands, wiped the girl's tears and said, "Now get the cards, we'll play gin and watch those birds get nice and fat."

She stood and turned to make tea and wiped away her own tears.

∞

The following Tuesday, Alexander and his wife Mihana arrived to help Mrs. Fitz organize, pack her belongings, and make arrangements for the rental of the house.

Clara couldn't bear the outright sale of the property. Her home was her creation song. Without it she would seize to exist.

Every morning when Clara rose out of bed her memories were renewed. What Clara forgot the house remembered. When she misplaced her children's laughter, the colors and smells of the garden brought it back. Once again, she could see her boys, seven and eight, rolling in the grass and running across the lawn. When the winter shadows of evening reached just so across her sitting room carpet she heard for a moment 16-year-old Alexander pushing open the front door and shaking the snow from his jacket, then running up the stairs to jovially harass his studious brother before dinner. Infant sons cried for her in the night, toddler boys crawled across the floor to retrieve balls under the chaise and roll them down the hall. In this house she didn't have two sons she had a hundred sons, a thousand sons of all ages.

This was the house that Charles had lived in. She would never stop seeing him coming up the walk toward her, arms outstretched. She would always feel him in the bed next to her. She would always smell him on her pillow.

Even when the memories faded the emotions would remain. Where would her joy come from without her home? How could she possibly put a price on these things? How would anyone even know what they were buying? She had to keep her home safe for her memories to live in. She had to believe she would come back. She would not sell.

∞

Mihana could not fully understand how Clara felt, but she sensed her distress. That week, while Alexander talked to movers and labeled boxes, Mihana, Clara and Chloe took pictures. They photographed Alexander's and Henry's rooms, complete with closeups of the beds, books and toys. They took pictures of the front hallway from the top of the stairs. The sitting room where Chloe had first awakened after her accident was well represented, as was the kitchen and the view from the kitchen window. They took an entire series of pictures of the garden and all its flowers with Chloe and Clara sitting at the garden table.

The day Clara finally drove away Chloe didn't leave her room. She didn't want to watch. She said her muffled good-byes the day before when the sun was still shining and everyone was taking pictures in the garden. She wasn't going with them. She wasn't part of that family.

Gloria no longer bothered with the day camp charade and went to work leaving Chloe home alone. It was a Friday and Dennis was picking her up from work and taking her to the Holiday Inn to relax. From there it would be dinner and dancing on the North Shore. Briefly Gloria wondered how he was paying for all this. He hadn't been doing well lately. She brushed her concern aside and relished the sudden upgrade in lodging. She left TV Dinners in the freezer.

Chloe sat at her desk that evening with her aluminum tray of peas and turkey before her. She picked at it absentmindedly as she looked out the window at the row of bushes between her and the garden. Her view of the bushes prevented her from seeing the asparagus patch, most of the old-fashioned roses and all of the fading blue and white campanulas. She could, however, clearly see the little white cast iron table and two lonely chairs standing in the twilight. By the end of the week even these would be invisible, packed away by the movers into the back of a padded van to travel hundreds of miles away to California. Chloe wanted to sit in her chair one last time.

She dropped the rest of her dinner tray into the waste basket, tied her sweater around her waist and left her house. The passageway through the bushes, narrow and almost impassable a few weeks earlier, was now easily traversed. The spiny branches had been parted so frequently that they had given up falling back into place. Chloe easily passed through unscathed with room to spare. She continued along the path she had made through the asparagus fronds, which were no longer soft and moist, but dry and prickly with the approach of autumn.

Chloe ran her hands over the back of the chairs and poked her fingers through the spaces between the metal leaves that formed the table top. She looked up at Mrs. Fitz' house and then focused on the back door. Her plans spontaneously changed.

The screen door swung aside easily. She turned the door knob and it responded with a click. To Chloe's relief it had been left unlocked for the movers who would arrive in the morning. She stepped inside. It was uncomfortably dim.

Chloe was afraid to turn on the lights. She didn't want to be discovered. She edged her way into the kitchen and reached for the flashlight that hung on the wall next to the telephone. She flipped it on and headed down the short hallway to the sitting room.

The beam from the flashlight acted as a beacon roaming the room in search of Clara. In the dim periphery the people in the photos no longer looked so friendly; the chaise where she first lay no longer appeared so cozy. She lowered herself into the chair at Clara's desk. It was cold and hard. Clara was not here.

She shined the light at her feet as she traveled under the raven who had returned after a long reprieve and was perched on the bookshelf near the doorway. He had given up waiting for a bust of Pallus or any other god or goddess of any real repute. He was just too tired to wait. He sat with his legs crossed and his feet dangling over the shelf. He cocked his head curiously at Chloe as she stopped to look up at him.

"Nevermore," he said to her.

"Nevermore," she replied.

She continued through the lifeless dining room and into the front entryway. The beam from the flashlight was drowned out by the headlights of a passing car which refracted through the cut glass, then traveled across the wall and part way up the stairs as the vehicle traveled on. Her shoes clicked on the stones as she proceeded to the stairs. She kicked them off at the bottom so she could feel her bare feet sink into the carpet as she ascended. At least this felt the same.

At the top of the stairs she turned into Alexander's room. She went directly to his desk and sat in his chair. In a moment she rose and went to the bookshelf. She leaned her back against it and shut her eyes as she rolled her body across the books to the opposite wall and then climbed onto the bed. She rolled over once and curled up tight, her arms clasped around her knees. Then she cried herself to sleep.

An hour later she awoke. Startled by her surroundings she pulled herself abruptly to the head of the bed and again clutched her knees tightly to her chest. Twilight had passed and night was upon her. City lights were now bright enough to shine in the windows and cast a dim and shadowy light throughout the house. When it dawned on her where she was she was no longer afraid. She stepped off the bed, walked out of the Alexander's room and proceeded down the hallway into Henry's room. Again she crawled up onto the bed, this time sitting on her knees at its head. She stood up in the center of the bed and plopped down cross legged. She stood again and allowed herself to fall back landing spread eagle, arms and legs out stretched. No matter what she tried she could not get comfortable. She climbed down and moved on.

She had never entered Clara's room before. She had looked in but never entered. She stepped over the threshold as if some mystical transformation might occur. It did not. The room was empty Clara's belongings were gone. Even the map of Japan above the bed, which Chloe now understood to be a gift from Mihana, had been rolled up and taken away. She lay on the stripped bed and looked at the ceiling. There was nothing here for her. Tucking the pillow under her arm she moved toward the door. Across the chair near the door was a discard lap blanket. She picked it up and left.

Once again in the hallway she dropped her bedding and pulled the rope to the attic. She looked up at the hole, dark and impenetrable above her and remembered the flashlight. It only took a moment to run back down the hall and retrieve it from Alexander's desk. Awkwardly she climbed the stairs to the attic dragging her bedding behind her. Then up the ladder she climbed, as she had done so many times before, and crawled clumsily onto the widow's walk. After propping the pillow in the corner against the railing she leaned back and looked out at the city at night.

∞

The house was dark when Gloria groggily turned her key in the lock and kicked her shoes off just inside the door. This was to be expected at one or two in the morning. Without bothering to turn on the lights she crossed the room by memory and touch until she came to the stairway. She counted the steps to eighteen, signaling her to continue down the hallway uninterrupted.

She was about to turn into her room and plunge gratefully between the covers when an uneasy feeling came over her. Something was different. Something wasn't right. After a brief internal conversation in which she tried to convince herself she was being ridiculous, she found herself unable to sleep. She sat up and grabbed her robe from the chair. Looping the tie around her waist she peeked out her doorway.

Nothing.

She went to the head of the stairway and peered down to the living room.

Again nothing.

Just as she was turning back into her room it dawned on her; Chloe's bedroom door was open. She could see the street light shining on the threadbare hall carpet. Chloe never slept with her door open.

Curious, she walked to Chloe's room and looked in.

Everything was impeccably in place except Chloe. Chloe was conspicuously absent.

"Chloe?" her mother called softly, as if she would come walking out of the closet at the sound of her name.

Gloria actually crossed the room and looked into the closet as if Chloe might be there at two o'clock in the morning. She was not.

After walking through the house calling Chloe all the way, Gloria went back to bed.

"She's spending the night at a friend's house," she lied to herself as she lay down. "She should have told me," She added grumpily.

She sat up again.

"Oh, come on!" she said to out loud this time. "We're talking about Chloe here. Chloe has no friends."

After that revelation Gloria's night was a mixed bag. She considered calling the police but thought about what they would say.

"She doesn't sound like a happy kid, Ma'am. Don't you think she's run away."

"She's got no place to run to sir."

"Well then she'll probably be home before morning. Kids are like that. We'll keep an eye out for her, but she'll be in bed before you wake up. Get some sleep now, Ma'am."

And off they'd go. Gloria didn't need the aggravation. She needed Chloe.

"She needed Chloe." What an odd thing to say, but it was true.

She slept for a few minutes mulling over this notion. She woke thinking of Hal. Then the voices started again.

"Had Chloe lost her mind? This was Chicago. You can't run away from home in Chicago as if it were some tiny burg on the prairie in the middle of nowhere."

At this point she began to feel the darkness weighing her down, crushing her into the bedding, smothering her in her own thoughts, causing her heart to alternately race out of control and stop stock still in her chest.

The memory of Hal crept back into her mind.

"Don't be ridiculous. This isn't Hal. This is Chloe. Chloe's fine. Nothing ever gets to Chloe. She can handle herself. She can handle anything," a voice reminded her firmly. "She will be in her bed when I wake up tomorrow."

But the other voice would not be stilled. That one whispered, "You'll be all alone." Then, "You need her," and finally, "I love her so much."

"Jesus, Chloe, where the hell are you?" she finally said out loud as again she sat up right in bed. Then it dawned on her.

When Gloria reached the Fitz' house the screen door was banging in the breeze and the back door itself was still open. Unlike Chloe, she had no reserves about turning on every light she could find. She had never been in any room other than the sitting room but she knew where she wanted to end up, and had a pretty good idea of how to get there. As she sped through the house she reached instinctively for the switches, leaving a trail of incandescence behind her. She took the stairs two at a time. When she reached the top, the attic staircase was hanging down, waiting for her at the end of the hall.

Gloria climbed into the dark hole above her and the stumbled and tripped across the attic toward the patch of light at the top of the ladder. Fortunately, Chloe had left the lid awry creating a guiding beam of light for Gloria. She clamored onto the roof to find her babe sleeping at her feet. Relief and vertigo swept over her. She fell to her knees.

After a few minutes she caught her breath, wiped the tears from her cheeks and leaned against the iron fence of the widow's walk next to Chloe. She curled up with Chloe in the crook of her arm and spread the blanket over them both. Beneath the blanket their bare feet entwined. For a moment Gloria wiggled her toes in a quiet caress.

In late August, at about 6 am, the street lights blink off and the buildings in Chicago begin to glow with the reflection of the rising sun. That's when Gloria awoke. She wasn't rested but she was awake. She looked out at the city. She saw the heat begin to rise. Streets and highways were filling with cars. The noise began to drift up to her. Everyone was going somewhere.

Looking out at the landscape, she could not picture any friends in the houses below. She could visualize no paths to success, feel no personal fulfillment. She had no future. In a few years she would have no Chloe. She was going nowhere.

She looked a little farther towards the horizon. The pink was disappearing from the sky behind her. A pair of jet trails crossed above her. In the distance she saw the lake. At least she thought she saw the lake. She watched a train as it traveled west. She felt like hell.

Chloe had been silently watching her mother for some time before Gloria looked down and saw her looking up.

"We're leaving here. Chloe," she said simply. "We're both going to run away."

13
EXIT DENNIS

It took Gloria just 3 weeks to sell the house. An eager young couple from Des Moines snatched it up fully furnished. In those three weeks Gloria managed to acquire a large black and blue mark on her hip from falling down the stairs; a variety of miscellaneous blemishes up and down her arms from general clumsiness and inattentiveness; and an unsightly bruise on her left cheek from walking into a door. Her lack of coordination was accompanied by a huge dip in self-esteem.

Dennis didn't show up for a week and a half after her "fall". He'd lost his job managing Best Used Cars, something about his inability to pinpoint a problem in the books. There had been a mention of jail time but nothing materialized. He had taken it out on Gloria, repeatedly. Now his time was being spent placating his panic-stricken wife and seeking new employment.

Gloria changed her hair color three times that first week but it didn't help her self-image or her balance. Both would have improved by changing the company she kept but the lower her self-esteem plunged the harder it was to be decisive. It was one more familiar path she had been down before but it took her well into the second week to recognize it. When she did she went back to being blonde, and when Dennis finally called she invited him to the Labor Day Picnic. She felt better already.

For a moment Gloria considered secretly inviting Dennis' wife to join them, but decided living with Dennis was probably enough punishment for her. Instead she sent her an FTD "Just For You" bouquet with a card reading "From Your Secret Admirer". She considered one that read "Condolences" but hoped the more romantic one would give Dennis something extra to think about.

Saturday was sweltering. Gloria kept the house locked up tight and the shades drawn in an attempt to keep the heat out and the cool of the previous night in. At about noon she tried another tack and opened all the doors and windows just enough to keep the air moving.

The smell of cigarette smoke wafted in through the screen door.

"Dennis is here," thought Chloe. Her stomach twisted both from the smell of cigarettes and from the thought of Dennis.

The bell rang.

Gloria was upstairs. Chloe lay silently on the couch with her book. An afternoon breeze swept in the window providing only a little relief from the heat. She could have gotten up or called for him to come in but she didn't. She could hear her mother walking along the upstairs hallway. Dennis would be in the house soon enough. She shut her book and sat up and watched her mother trip lightly down the staircase in her red and white tube top and short shorts. The navy-blue sash she had tied around her waist waived patriotically.

Gloria opened the front door. Dennis stood before her in his multicolored tropical shirt and Bermuda shorts, hair slicked back and nails trimmed. A gold chain swung freely about his neck. He was ready to whisk Gloria off her feet as if nothing unusual had happened between them. His ego knew no bounds.

Chloe, of course, was not included in his afternoon plans. He dismissed her with a distracted nod, never taking his eyes off the bouncing tube top.

"Hey, Hot Stuff," he said as he slipped his arm around Gloria's waist and buried his face in her neck. His eyes looked up over her shoulder and glared at Chloe to get lost.

Chloe, nauseated, got up to leave.

Gloria laughed and slipped out of Dennis' grasp. He followed her into the living room.

"Listen, Dennis, I have something to tell you," said Gloria in a slightly uneasy tone.

Chloe's heart fluttered. She stopped on the bottom step of the staircase with her hand on the banister. Curiosity had gotten the better of her. She turned to watch.

Dennis looked at them both apprehensively.

"We're leaving Chicago. We're going to California, Gloria announced decisively.

Dennis' ruddy complexion instantly turned the color of Pompeian ash. He made a variety of choking and sputtering noises. His eyes widened and narrowed in rapid succession as he desperately searched for the appropriate words, of which, of course, there were none. He sounded as if he had swallowed a toad.

"We can't," he croaked. He looked furtively around the room and began walking in small circles. His personal scenario of this relationship suddenly contained a large black hole. His eyes fixed on the door for a moment and then back on Gloria.

"We can't go anywhere," he sputtered. "I have a wife. I'm married. I can't leave her. She needs me."

Dennis' reality was dissolving around him. Those nights in the back of the car, the afternoons at the nature preserve and ahhh... that time at the holiday inn, were all being sucked into the black hole at lightning speed. There went the lace brazier...the red panties...the piggy mask, all right, loose that...but oh, not the black stiletto heels with the little ankle straps....

Beads of sweat were rapidly collecting on his brow and began dripping into his eyes. He wiped them aside with his handkerchief and stepped back. Instinctively he pulled a chair between himself and Gloria as a barricade to the inevitable hysterical barrage that was forthcoming in response to the devastating psychological blow he had just dealt.

The stillness in the room was comparable to that in a cathedral after the tones of the lowest and largest bells have stopped ringing. No one breathed. Then the little bells chimed in. Gloria and Chloe were laughing uncontrollably.

"Not we," said Gloria with a circular motion of her hands indicating herself and Dennis. "We," she reiterated repeating the motion to indicate only herself and Chloe.

Dennis, stunned, dropped into the easy chair and stared into space. They were leaving him.

"Get the man a glass of water, Chloe," directed Gloria. She reconsidered. "Get two."

Dennis was completely baffled by the utter lack of concern Gloria had expressed over his earth-shaking confession. And now this… this betrayal. How could she leave him…him!

His mind jerked back to the word "wife". My God what had he said? He tensed. Perhaps "glass of water" was a code between those two for "pistol in the silverware drawer". His plans for fried chicken and hot sex were not materializing. Red lights began flashing in his head.

"Run away. Run away. Run away," repeated his inner voice. "Escape. Escape. Flee!"

Chloe handed her mother a tumbler of water and kept one for herself. She had understood the code. Gloria gave Dennis his refreshments in the face. A sweet little smile swept over Chloe's face as she stepped forward simultaneously and, quickly but cautiously, flung the second glass in his lap.

The water to the groin caused Dennis to sharply inhale a mouthful of the water to the face. Now he was choking in earnest. Chloe and Gloria were appropriately unconcerned. Together they pulled him from the chair and shoved him out the door.

"It's been really fun," said Gloria. "Thanks for everything. See you around."

They stood outside in the sun for a moment, watching as Dennis, still shaking the water from his hair and clothes, stumbled toward his car.

"By the way, Dennis," she called after him, "Your wife is the best thing that ever happened to me."

Happy to find himself sans bullet holes and still in complete possession of all of his body parts, Dennis departed muttering in a bewildered voice, a variety of colorful clichés and quaint colloquialisms.

Gloria stood on the front steps with her hands on her hips. Her eyes followed the departing vehicle as it squealed out of the driveway and down the street.

"Get the boxes from the attic, Chloe," said Gloria. "It's time to pack."

14

ON THE ROAD

Some people make a big deal out of the difference between running away and running to. Actually, the difference is negligible. The important thing is often that you go. Sometimes running away is just what the doctor ordered.

Two weeks into September, Chloe and Gloria packed their last two bags, tossed them in the trunk of the Bel Aire, threw blankets and pillows in the back seat and made for the Dan Ryan Expressway going south. Gloria didn't so much as glance over her shoulder as they drove off. Chloe began to turn but Gloria directed her attention to adjusting the radio.

"Find WLS," she instructed, "We can listen to that all the way to Omaha."

By the time Chloe's head bobbed back up their house had slipped out of sight.

Both Gloria and Chloe had felt a certain amount of trepidation as the actual day of departure drew near. Sitting side by side on the Bel Aire's white, faux leather, bench seat staring at America for 2,000 miles would be about as personal as Gloria and Chloe had ever gotten. Gloria wondered what the two of them would talk about for 30 hours in the car. Chloe wasn't so optimistic as to expect any conversation at all. Eventually they both modified their expectations. Gloria had Danny at the 66 Station put loud speakers in the car as a buffer between herself and complete and total silence. Chloe made flash cards of subjects that might spark communication between them. Short introductory statements were written in small print in the right hand corner of each. They included:

The sky ~ "I don't think I've ever seen such a (pretty, colorful, stormy, dark, gloomy) (sunset, sun rise, morning, afternoon, evening) have you?"

The road ~ "I wonder where this road (goes, starts, stops, narrows, becomes paved again)"

California ~ "What do you suppose is the most important (crop, import, export, manufactured product) of California?"

In a moment of unthwarted cynicism she added:

Sleazy men I've known and haven't slept with. A good subject if Chloe felt like talking and her mother felt like being silent or...

Unfamiliar places I've slept without a toothbrush. An interesting topic if Gloria felt eloquent and Chloe needed a break.

After half an hour she had a stack of fifteen topics. They ranged from world geography to favorite foods.

"Off into the wild blue yonder," Gloria declared cheerfully as they pulled out of the driveway.

Chloe tucked her 4x4 cards into the pocket of the door on the passenger side for easy access. Then she pulled out the copy of Tennyson that Clara had given her that last day in the garden. The rhythm of the six hundred ill-fated men marching into the valley of death made a nice counterpoint to the erratic sound of the tires as they struck each break in the concrete of the on ramp

"Kudos, Gloria," Gloria said out loud as she glanced at herself in the rear view mirror and slipped on her sunglasses.

An hour later she turned off the radio and stopped for gas. 33.9 / gallon. Free set of picnic cups with a full tank. She and Chloe took turns at the bathroom while the attendant filled the tank, washed the windows and put the box of picnic cups in the back seat. She let him keep the change for his trouble. The full 53 cents. She was feeling magnanimous.

By 11:00 the two reached Moline and the initial excitement of the adventure had ebbed. Gloria turned up the radio and made a mental note to send a postcard of heartfelt gratitude to Danny at the 66 Station as soon as they reached Omaha. He probably had no idea how much she appreciated his work. She recalled his charming smile and willingness to please. A nice characteristic in one so young. Nice shoulders, too, from what she could ascertain by the way his sleeveless t-shirt stretched across his chest. She paused a moment to enjoy that memory. Beautiful hands for a mechanic. Clean and slender. Nails well kept. Well, he wasn't really a mechanic, he worked in electronics.

Chloe on the other hand had just drifted off to sleep. When she first shut her eyes she drew a meticulous image of Walden Pond, as she decided it should be, on the pure and untouched canvas of her mind. She imagined tranquil waters with rushes growing to the left. A swan drifted across the pond beneath blue skies where cotton ball clouds passed silently overhead. There was a mossy patch next to the reeds inviting her to enter the picture and she sat there for a while until the tranquility was more than she could bear. On her left, a fiery red maple sprouted instantly up to full height. It pleased her. Around its trunk cluster of red sumac bush rustled in all its autumn glory. Then, out of the sumac, jumped a boy, dark skinned and laughing. It was Mogli! Monkeys appeared in the leaves of the maple and began to shriek. The sumac turned to flames. Out of the flames appeared not Mogli but Kammel on horseback. The horse reared up and whinnied as he turned and galloped across the plain. Chloe was no longer seated by the water but riding behind Kammel, galloping across the plains with him, arms clinging tightly around his waist, galloping, galloping....

Then she dreamed of soft bunnies.

When Chloe finally awoke it was raining hard. The wipers shoved the water across the windshield and it streaked back across her window making it hard to see out. Through the blur she could see a sodden expanse of wheat bent over in the fields from the weight of a future harvest and more water than it could support. The honey blonde of the wheat fields alternated with the velvety black loam of alfalfa fields already turned and planted with winter wheat.

"Where are we?"

"Almost to Nebraska," came the reply. "You missed Iowa. There was corn. Don't worry, I'm sure there will be more coming up soon."

"Ah, there it is now," she said, pointing out ahead.

"I see," said Chloe. "Did I miss anything else?"

"No," said her mother, "just corn and wheat. A couple more gas stations. Are you all right? You slept forever."

"Ya," said Chloe, "but my stomach is kind of upset."

"Maybe you should eat something," said her mother. "I'm hungry too. We'll stop as soon as we see someplace."

When they pulled up to The Rattlesnake Bar and Grill the rain had stopped. They stepped from the car and slogged through the mud.

"What *is* that smell?" asked Chloe.

"Agriculture," said her mother. "Wet dirt and cows."

She nodded towards half a dozen of the creatures standing in the mire next to the fence.

"Makes me gag," she added.

Tufts of fur were tangled in the barbed wire. The top half of each cow was washed clean by the rain, the bottom half was crusted with mud and dirt where it had plopped down in the field during the storm.

"I don't really think it's that bad," said Chloe. "It's kind of fresh smelling." She was trying to be open minded, trying to embrace new experiences.

"Makes me gag," said Gloria again, scrapping the soles of her shoes on the concrete step.

Chloe reached for the door.

The rust had been dripping for years from the screw that attached the wooden handle to the torn screen door. The orange line it left extended in a jagged pattern through the peeling paint. Apparently, the door had been green at one time, white before that, and possibly yellow or brown before that. Chloe opened the door, then paused on the doorstep having second thoughts about leading the way into this questionable excuse for a diner. She could see that it was just a bar that sold hot dogs with the beer.

Gloria gave her a push and the two found themselves standing inside The Rattlesnake.

"Find a table. I'm going to the bathroom," said Gloria.

Obediently Chloe sat down in the closest chair she could find and tried to move the curtain in the window enough to look out. It couldn't be done. The curtain was attached at both the top and the bottom to prevent any contact with the outside world. This encouraged the customers to continue drinking and playing pool endlessly without any ugly references to solar time.

Chloe picked up her napkin and began fraying the edge to keep herself occupied. She had never been a nervous child before but that could easily change. She had never sworn before either, but with any extended exposure to establishments like this that, too, could come about. Expletives spurted from the area around the pool table like lava from Vesuvius and rained down on her mercilessly.

"Where was her mother?" her brain began to shriek. She resisted the urge to curl up in the fetal position under the table. One glance at the floor and that course of action was clearly out of the question.

"Where the Hell was her mother" was the phrase that next came to mind. Chloe was a quick learner.

Her vocabulary lesson was abruptly interrupted by the nameless horror that slipped into the seat across from her, the seat that should have by now been occupied by her ever-so-tardy mother. He composed himself by combing his unkempt hair back with his fingers, somehow expecting that the grime from his hands and nails would increase his good looks. He licked the drool from the corner of his grinning mouth and tossed his best pickup line on the table for Chloe to snatch up.

"Hi there little lady'" he crooned reaching his big, weathered, scabby hand across the table towards her childish pink one.

Her hand retracted as if it were on a spring and her discomfort level shot through the roof. Her eyes kept moving from the man's missing teeth to the glass eyes of the stuffed antelope mounted directly above him.

She stared at him, speechless.

"I was over there making my shot," he continued, nodding backward toward the motley crew at the pool table behind him. "Couldn't hardly concentrate with you looking so cute over here. You and me, let's get in the truck and go shoot ourselves some prairie dogs. Bring some beers. Me and my buddy got fifty-seven last Friday. Had a blast. Ya wanna?"

Chloe's blood instantly drained from her face. She remembered to breathe just before passing out. She knew no answer to encompass how she felt about that offer. She rose abruptly and searched for the door. It wasn't hard to spot, it was the only source of natural light in the haze of cigarette smoke and green phosphorescence.

"Leaving NOW," she said to her mother as she passed her coming out of the door marked "heifers". The tattered screen door slammed behind her as she headed for the car.

"Come back inside, Chloe. I've got to take a break," said Gloria exhausted. "I'm not driving another inch without a break."

"Get me out of here," Chloe demanded.

"If we leave now you'll have to drive," Gloria responded, as if the absurdity of that statement would put an end to the argument.

"Sounds good to me," replied Chloe.

"Don't be ridiculous, you don't know how."

"So teach me. You're my mother. Try teaching me something... nursery rhymes... long division... how to bake a cake... anything! It's what mother's do!" shouted Chloe for the first time in her life.

She turned her back on her mother to hide the unexpected look of delight that had taken possession of her face. She struggled to hold on to her anger in spite of the revelation that it was deliciously fun expressing it.

Gloria paused, mulling this idea over for a moment. This was Nebraska, how hard could it be to teach a kid to drive in Nebraska. She could sleep. Why not?

"I'll get the hot dogs, she said.

"A salad, too," said Chloe, unrealistically.

When Gloria returned Chloe was propped up on books and sweaters, revving up the engine and ready to go. Gloria handed her a hot dog and an orange soda through the window. She continued around to the passenger side still balancing a hot dog, two salads (surprise), a bag of chips and a drink under her chin. Setting her drink on the rooftop Gloria opened the door and started handing the rest of the food to Chloe while climbing inside.

"Ready?" asked Chloe.

"Eat" responded Gloria, reaching out the window to retrieve her drink from the roof.

"I'll eat while I drive," said Chloe brightly. "You do."

"Not on your life," Gloria said. "I'm not interested in ending up back in Chicago on the grill of an oncoming cattle truck."

Gloria instructed while they ate.

"All you need to know for starters is the gas pedal and the break. Use your right foot for both."

"What are you saving your left foot for?" asked Chloe.

"I don't really know. That's just the way you do it." replied Gloria.

Rejecting her mother's advice, Chloe lurched down the highway, left foot on the break and right foot on the gas, with Gloria yelling "stop!" over and over again as orange soda and mustard flew all over the interior of her car.

"Well that explains it," said Gloria, pulling her fingernails out of the arm rest. There's a reason for the left foot-right foot rule. She gave up on the rest of her meal, and on her clothes, which were irreparably stained. Chloe continued experimenting with various speeds and means of controlling them while Gloria removed her clothes down to her underwear and used them to wipe off the dash. She considered replacing them with something from her suitcase but it was in the trunk so she forwent the formality of dressing and leaned back to enjoy the ride. It was an unusually hot and humid September.

Trusting that a smart girl like Chloe would certainly be OK at the wheel without her, she closed her eyes and was asleep instantly. Fortunately, she was right. Chloe resumed the parental role, which over the past months, she had become relatively familiar with. Hoping her mother might sleep for the rest of the trip, Chloe amused herself for the next half hour trying to remember everything she'd ever read about India. Another half hour was spent considering birds and the nature of flight.

It was about two in the afternoon when the air thickened and the clouds dropped down from above. They rapidly evolved from a boring, flat, dirty gray cloud cover that could suck the joy from the most carefree ride, to a truly ominous, black, multidimensional demon of a cloud cover that could crush the life out of you if it came any closer to the ground. A rapid, unexpected temperature drop awoke Gloria with a shiver, but what really stood her hair on end was the funnel cloud making matchsticks of the water tower about 200 yards in front of them. Then it was gone.

Although somewhat terror stricken herself, Chloe recovered quickly enough to fully appreciate her mother's horror. She was delighted by this little bit of revenge provided on her behalf by the Mother Nature for the innumerable wrongs she had endured at her mother's hand. After her wicked little pleasure passed she felt oddly closer to her mother.

Chloe pulled the car over onto the shoulder waited for her mother to stop babbling.

"Oh, my God, Oh, my God, Oh, my God..." was all Gloria could say.

Just then the Nebraska State Trooper pulled up behind them and lumbered up to the driver's side window.

"You two all right?" he asked as he leaned down, hand on his mighty 44 Magnum, to assess the situation.

"Yes Sir," said Chloe, trying to look as tall as possible to hide her age and as wide as possible to hide her naked mother.

"We're fine officer," chimed in Gloria who had never felt at a loss with her clothes off before and didn't intend to now.

When the Officer saw Chloe sitting on her books he astutely surmised that she was not a legal operator of a motor vehicle even if you factored in the possibility that this Bel Aire was being used for agricultural transport, which it clearly wasn't.

However, the longer he conversed with her mother the less sure he became of his initial perceptions. Perhaps Chloe was older than she looked. Maybe there were chickens in the trunk. Anything was possible. He strolled around to the passenger window to discuss it with Gloria, who, from the looks of her, was clearly a very grown-up girl.

"Honestly, Officer. It has been so hard for her, looking so young and all. You can imagine how difficult it is for her to date when boys are always looking for someone, well you no," she said as she shimmied her near-naked upper body.

The Officer was becoming more and more sympathetic.

"...and she's so smart, aren't you Chloe? Anybody this smart is clearly old enough to drive. Show the man how smart you are Chloe. Recite something for him."

Chloe's brief moment of inner reconciliation with her mother passed instantly. Frantically she struggled to choose a piece of verse that would save them both.

All she could come up with was Blake:

Tygre, tygre, burning bright
In the forest of the night,
What immortal hand or eye
Could frame thy fearful symmetry?
In what distant deeps or skies...

She would have continued but her mother cut her off.

'There, you see,' Gloria interrupted. "and so religious, too. She recites only verses about God. I'm so proud of her," said Gloria as she squeezed her arms together with joy, causing her buxom breasts to balloon over the top of her bra.

The Trooper could not readily sort out where God was in the recitation, but he surmised it must have something to do with the immortal part. At any rate he summarily dismissed what either Chloe or Gloria were saying in favor of what he was actually seeing, bouncing right there in front of him. By now he was sure Chloe was at least sixteen, but there was the matter of a license, just for the record.

"But the storm, Officer. It was terrible. We were so frightened. And the wind came and sucked everything out of the car. All our identification. Everything. Our hats, our purses, everything. I mean, just look at me. Do you think I drive around like this everyday. It was a horrible."

The officer took a long, long look at her.

In the end the police report read something like this:

Officer came to the assistance of two white females stranded by high winds and rain. Threshing machine with trailer driven by twenty-two year old midget accompanied by her sister. Officer calmed the women. Two cows and a pig unharmed.

After the tornado passed and the trooper departed, the chill in the air prompted Gloria to pop the trunk and drag a suitcase into the backseat to look for a clean set of clothes. She took the driver's seat fully clad, just in case her trooper friend alerted his comrades to the peep show. Men certainly like to talk and she wasn't interested in improvising an encore.

After hours of cruising along thoroughly fed up with America's Breadbasket, Gloria and Chloe longed in earnest for a brief stretch of apple orchards or even a lone pine; possibly a tall apartment building with lots of noisy smelly cars in the parking lot, or a strip mall with long lines of people waiting to get into a movie that had been sold out but no one had gotten the message. Anything to relieve the tedium of corn and wheat.

Nary an apple nor a cone came into sight. The view went from fields to sky without interruption. Conversation had run out miles ago and Chloe's cards had slipped out of reach under her seat. Entertainment of any kind would have been welcomed but the prospects looked grim.

This time it was Chloe who switched on the radio but she switched it off again immediately, unable to cope with the afternoon of nasal acrobatics this part of the country had to offer. As hard as she tried, she could not help but think of home, well, not her home, actually, but Clara's home, sitting in the garden reading poetry and telling stories.

"Tell me a story," she blurted out unexpectedly.

"Honestly Chloe. You're too old for stories." Gloria replied without a moment's hesitation. "Any way, I don't tell stories. Never been any good at it. Do you have any gum?"

"Oh please," Chloe pleaded. "I am so bored. If you tell me one I'll tell you one. What else have we got to do? And no I don't"

They reached the end of the cornfield. Across the fence another sprang up immediately. Every ten or fifteen minutes they passed an oncoming pickup truck or an occasional station wagon.

"I don't know any stories," her mother said with one hand on the wheel and the other rummaging around in her purse searching for the Doublemint.

"Of course you do," Chloe insisted. "Someone must have told you stories when you were little."

For Chloe it had not been her mother but her kindergarten teacher at Washington Elementary who read to the class every afternoon over the sound of the El rattling through their rest period. For an instant, she saw miss Hogan seated in the back seat of the Bel Aire peering over a minuscule Little Golden Book. Chloe reflected on what a good year five had been and intensely mourned her lost youth. No one ever really appreciates their youth until it's gone.

Gloria found her gum and ignored Chloe while she struggled to unwrap it with her teeth. The heat had fused the sticky mess to the wrapper and when she was finally able to chew it a tiny fleck of foil lodged in her filling causing her to swerve off the road, crushing a sleeping snake and frightening a multitude of noisy, flying grasshoppers to their death on her windshield.

The long stretch of silence caused Chloe to give up on any chance of stories. She turned to look out the window and tried to think of the word "corn" in as many languages as she could. Corn was all she could come up with. They didn't teach foreign languages in grade school.

"V daleekoy strane," said her mother.

Chloe looked quizzically at her mother, who was apparently speaking in tongues. Too many strange religious ceremonies for this woman, she thought to herself.

"V daleekom tsare," continued Gloria. "v gloobokom tyemnom, dzeel Babba Yagga. That's how my grandfather told it."

For Chloe's benefit she started again in English.

"In a country far away, in a tzardom far away, in a deep dark forest, lived Babba Yagga," began Gloria.

Then she filled Chloe's head with a menagerie of characters: a house with eyes who pranced around on chicken legs, a witch who traveled in a flying teacup, and myriad characters who risked being eaten if they didn't watch their step in the deep, dark forests on the banks of the Don in the Ukraine.

"There are a lot of Babba Yagga stories," explained Gloria. "They're Slavic. My grandparents told them all the time."

"Where were your parents?" Chloe asked. It was a question she'd thought about but never before dared ask.

"Worked for Hormel. Died for Spam," said Gloria, who immediately turned on the radio to mark the end of that discussion. All communication abruptly seized. No additional stories followed. Some tortured female wailed at them but no effort was made to stop her pain. Chloe had no idea what had transpired. They had been doing so well. What went wrong? She longed to talk. Where were the cards? Panic crept in. She would have to improvise.

"Do you know," Chloe asked brightly, "from what direction the predominant winds come from in Utah?"

Even Chloe recognized this as a pathetic effort. A clear act of desperation. Who *would* know from what the direction the predominant winds came from in Utah? And why would they care?

There was no response.

Gloria had not even heard the question.

"Misha," she was thinking. That's what they had called her, and Gloria missed them.

15

BA-BOOM

They passed through Oglallah and then Fort Sedgewick, which appeared to be more of a gas station than a fort. Gloria pulled over. Denver or Cheyenne? Wyoming or Colorado? They sat up in their seats and scanned the landscape for any hint of the majestic Rocky Mountains they had heard so much about. Dry grasslands abounded but there was not even a hill in sight.

"I don't know which way, Chloe," her mother repeated, getting increasingly irritated by the question. "I didn't know the first time you asked and I don't know now."

She was fumbling with the map which she had given up trying to refold the last time she'd used it when, in her frustration, she had wadded it up in a ball and stuffed it in the glove compartment like a vicious little animal in a cage.

"I can't believe we headed across this entire United States and you don't even know where we're going!" Chloe was yelling now. She was a stickler for direction in every sense of the word and the loss of the same caused her to act her age, something she had rarely before done. She threw her hands in the air and looked up at the heavens, well actually at the roof of the car but her theatrical flare implied the heavens.

She found her own performance surprisingly uplifting. This new Chloe, the one who had first emerged at Bud's Bar and Grill, had escaped again.

Gloria began to feel irresponsible and guilty, two emotions she was relatively unfamiliar with. All this driving was affecting her. She recovered almost immediately.

"Get out," she said abruptly.

Chloe just looked at her.

"Now!" said her mother sharply. She was staring straight ahead.

Chloe opened the door and looked down for a moment at the scrappy little weeds that were growing up in the gravel where the shoulder of the road thinned out into dirt, then into tall, dry grass and thistle. She stepped out, slammed the door defiantly, and turned her back towards the car. She waited for Gloria to join her and to lecture her on the value of respect after which they would both apologize, spread the map on the hot, dusty hood of the automobile and decide what to do next. That's the way she imagined people handled this kind of thing.

To her horror she heard of the sound of the tires spitting out dry gravel, then jumping back onto the asphalt and speeding away. She turned her head just in time to see Gloria, disappearing down the highway without looking back.

Chloe was stunned. What had she done? She wasn't very good at this mother-daughter thing. Apparently, she had ruined everything. She fought back the tears until her nose began to run. Her knees gave out and she sat down in the tall grass. Milkweed fluff stuck to her hair and nettles burned the back of her knees.

Gloria reached a stand of cottonwoods near an irrigation ditch and pulled the car over, out of sight. There she sat for four or five minutes, secure in the knowledge that Chloe could go nowhere without her.

She slowly pulled the car back to the edge of the trees and peered through the branches to watch her daughter. It was Gloria's turn to be horrified. Chloe was gone.

Gloria exploded out of the car and into the middle of the road. Frantically she scanned the roadside for any glimpse of Chloe. There was not a soul in sight.

In an instant she leaped back into her seat, whipped the car around and raced back down the highway to the point she had last seen her daughter. She didn't spot the navy blue sneakers sticking out of the weeds until she nearly ran over them. Leaning hard on the brakes Gloria cruised right past Chloe at a deceptively moderate pace effectively disguising her terror. A few yards down the road she composed herself and made a quick u-turn. The car rolled to a halt. Chloe rose to her feet.

Chloe saw her mother's long, bare arm stretch across the front seat and fling the door open nearly cracking Chloe in the knees.

"Get in," Gloria ordered.

Chloe obeyed.

"I'm the boss," Gloria said in a cold and piercing voice, without even looking at Chloe. Her eyes never strayed from some hypothetical spot far beyond the windshield.

Chloe nodded, saying nothing

"The correct answer is "yes, ma'am.""

"Yes," said Chloe, choking on her words. "Ma'am," she added, with tears running down her hot, pink cheeks.

"Good," said Gloria. "We're going to Colorado. I want to see the mountains."

With that she veered sharply left onto the pavement and shortly down the road turned onto highway 40.

Chloe stared out the window silently counting telephone poles as they whizzed by

1……2…..3….

Then 4..5..6..

They were picking up speed.

7,8,9,10,11

She was still breathing in little gasps.

Gloria was unable to remain detached.

"You must have known I was coming back," she said.

It was a statement, false actually, that Chloe was, at this moment, unable to respond to.

35, 36 she counted silently while Gloria spoke. It kept the lump from forming too tightly in her throat, which by now was sore from inhaling dust and swallowing tears.

50, 51.. 52... 53......54

Gloria was not an much of a multitasker. She slowed down and pulled off the road to talk. When she turned to face Chloe, no words came to mind. Finally, she said, "Do you want to drive?"

Chloe nodded.

∞

The moment the car started the ascent into the foothills Chloe knew something was wrong. Half an hour later she pulled over and threw up. For most people being at the wheel of the automobile relieves motion sickness but with a good dose of altitude sickness to boot, Chloe was helpless. She nudged her mother, who resisted opening her eyes so soon.

Gloria muttered from deep inside her mental cocoon, "What is it, Chloe?"

"I'm sick," said Chloe.

"No, you're not," responded Gloria flatly.

"Yes, I am," Chloe whispered, afraid to open her mouth any wider.

Gloria's eyes were now creeping open of their own accord. There was no denying it, Chloe looked terrible.

"Dramamine" said Gloria. "You need Dramamine. Stop at the next town. We'll get some."

She put her head back and dozed off again. A moment later she sensed something missing. There was a decided lack of acceleration.

Reluctantly she rolled her head to the side and squinted in Chloe's direction. Chloe was no longer at the wheel. She had crawled into the back seat and was curled up asleep.

Gloria dragged herself from the car, stretched her limbs in all directions, and was suddenly bowled over by the magnificence of the Gore Range. These were not the foothills. Gloria had actually been sleeping for hours and Chloe had miraculously made it to the base of Berthoud Pass.

∞

"It's a long way to Tipparareeee, It's a long way to go…" chirped Gloria as they careened up and down the mountainside.

An hour had passed since Chloe's last dose of Dramamine. They had picked some up at a gas station. Apparently, it was a best seller.

"I'm going to be sick again," she moaned.

"Here," her mother said as she pulled the purple cellophane box from her pocket one more time and passed it to Chloe. "Take some more Dramamine. You can't be sick now. Look at this! Snow-capped peaks. Purple mountains' majesty. Beautiful for spacious skies! Pull yourself together!"

"This is so unfair," Chloe moaned. "This is made for me. It's what I've always wanted." Of course, she moaned this to herself. Almost everything she said now she said to herself. Force of necessity. She wanted to make no more mistakes. She needed to update her cue cards.

"Pull over!" she blurted out before she could down the pill.

The car stopped abruptly and Chloe rolled out onto the tundra. She dragged herself a few feet and threw up on the handmade sign that pleaded for the preservation of the fragile alpine environment. "Berthoud Pass 11,113 feet," said the sign next to it. She briefly regretted the destructive trail she had blazed to her present position in the scrub oak. All those little lichen, lost forever. When she looked up at the vast expanse of snowy peaks her remorse dissolved into wonder. She swallowed hard and the pill struck home.

"Let's stay here. Why go any farther?" she asked her mother. She knew Thoreau would love it. The air couldn't get much thinner.

"Of course," responded her mother, " and when winter comes and I don't have a job I'll just have to eat you." The last gas station they passed through had brochures on Alfred Packer, who had cannibalized other members of his party while snowbound in 1874.

Also," she added reaching into the car through the open window and pulling out her sweater, " it's mid-September. Look out there. There's snow on the ground. Kind of bodes ill for October through June, I'd say."

"Point taken," conceded Chloe. "Let's go to the beach. California or bust. Where's the Dramamine?"

They stopped for Dramamine in Kremmling. They stopped for Dramamine in Steamboat Springs. They stopped for Dramamine in Rifle, where they bought the Dramamine at the Smith and Wesson Drug, which stood next to the Shotgun Bar, which was next to an all-night establishment called Guns and Buns. Occasionally they stopped for snacks to buffer the Dramamine. Between stops Chloe read aloud to Gloria the pamphlet inside the Dramamine package, searching for information on the lives of Dramamine junkies. Would she have withdrawal symptoms in Utah? Would she have to rob banks in Nevada to support her habit? What sort of ugly, sordid life lay ahead for a Dramamine junkie?"

The strongest warning she found clearly advised not operating heavy equipment while eating Dramamine like breakfast cereal. Heavy equipment, in relationship to a ten-year-old, undoubtedly included automobiles. Consequently, Chloe missed most of Colorado riding shotgun in a Dramamine stupor while her mother remained glued to the wheel.

As they climbed Muddy Pass traffic as well as air thinned. Empty carcasses of once vigorous vehicles littered the shoulder of the road. Oxygen starved automobiles stalled and died a sad and sordid death. The smell of burning oil was in the air. Stranded motorists held their thumbs to the sky but Gloria, not wanting to become one of the fallen, passed them by on her way to the summit of Rabbit Ears Pass.

Blinding rain began around 8,000 feet and settled down to a steady drizzle at 9,000. The car veritably skated across the expanse from Muddy Pass to Rabbit Ears Pass. Brilliant fall colors were awash in rain and sleet, and thick clouds hid the intensely blue skies. These were not the depressing, low hanging, grey clouds of the Midwest, the ones that the pair could have stood on their tiptoes and touched with their fingertips. At the top of Rabbit Ears Pass the clouds hung at their feet, engulfed them, and swirled about them. They washed over their faces and entered their bodies, tickling their throats and filling both hearts and lungs with a wet emptiness. Little wisps competed for attention, appearing and disappearing at their own whim. The atmosphere was refreshingly, piercingly, gloomy.

They crested the summit. The valley below was beyond beautiful, it was stunning, even more so for its wet, rich colors. Through the enormous, dripping pines Gloria glimpsed a dark, shimmering lake below and was tempted to veer left into oncoming traffic for a better look. The sound of the trucker leaning on his horn startled her back to her senses.

Chloe slept on, oblivious to it all.

Far below, the pink neon rabbit in front of the Rabbit Ears Motel resembled Bugs Bunny more than any respectable western jack rabbit. The only thing missing was the carrot. The resemblance was lost on Chloe, who never opened her eyes as her mother led her to their room. Gloria tipped Chloe over onto the pillow and pulled the covers over her chin just before she walked out the door. It didn't occur to her to leave a note. She told Marg at the front desk she could be found across the street at the hot springs pool, if Chloe should ask.

Waking up alone in a strange hotel room was not a happy experience for Chloe. She reasoned that in all likelihood her mother had not abandoned her, but she wasn't entirely sure. She sat on the edge of the bed in the dark and told herself Kipling's story, "The Elephant's Child". The feisty little elephant marched all the way from Graham's Town to Kimberley...to the great, grey-green, greasy Limpopo River. He had a bit of a run in with a crocodile but in the end got to smack the tar out of everyone that had mistreated him, including his parents and a couple of orangutans. For that reason, Chloe always thought that, although it was a bit childish, it was one of Kipling's best.

By the time the little elephant had administered his last spanking Gloria was still not back. Quietly Chloe rose off the bed and picked up the room key from the table near the door, pausing for a moment to look at herself in the mirror. There her own face was joined on either side by the horse heads reflected from the pictures that hung over each bed behind her. It made a strange triumvirate. The lamp on the table was made of a worn and reworked cowboy boot. She flipped off the switch attached to the pointed toe and stepped outside.

Chloe found herself standing in the parking lot with a yellow bug light directly over her head. It made her bare arms and legs look sallow and gruesome. She turned a strange pink as she approached the rabbit sign outside the office.

Inside Marg directed her to the hot spring pools across the street. Chloe took one glimpse of Gloria up to her armpits in steamy water and steamier men and went back to bed, secure in the knowledge that her mother would be somewhere in the vicinity all night and back to drive by dawn. It was some consolation anyway.

That night she dreamed an elephant stepped on her mother.

∞

"Just buy the gas mother," Chloe pleaded as they got closer.

"Not on your life," replied Gloria indignantly. "Last gas for 150 miles. What a lot of baloney. False advertising is what that is. 150 miles! That's ridiculous," she proclaimed and went on driving. "I've got half a tank of gas. We can go for almost 100 miles on that."

Chloe turned and watched uneasily as the Last Chance Gas and Grill rapidly disappearing behind them. A giant flashing neon mud flap girl riding a bucking bronco on the roof waved at them repetitiously with her pink cowboy hat as they left.

An hour later Chloe tried to peek inconspicuously over at the gas gauge for the third time. Her mother glared at the road ahead and said tersely, "knock it off Chloe. There'll be a gas station in a minute. It can't possibly be much farther."

"Rock to the right, rock to the left and low lean thorn between," Chloe began to recite silently. She could never remember any of the church prayers, though god knows she had heard enough of them. Negative associations erased them from her mind immediately after each amen. Kipling, on the other hand was always comforting. The Khyber Pass replaced the Valley of the Shadow of Death quite effectively. Horses hooves drummed through Chloe's dehydrated little head as she vaguely wondered if Kipling had really been passing through Utah rather than India when he wrote his poem.

"East is east and west is west and never the twain shall meet..." the voice in her head continued. The rhythm throbbed in her brain.

The words were now spoken in a godlike voice booming from the "bush to the left", as it burst into flames. Breech bolts snicked to beat the band.

She awoke in a sweat and peeled her back from the plastic seat as she sat up.

She had had a vision, she was sure. It was warning her that she should never have left home.

Chloe felt the desert just wasn't up to snuff. She had been expecting something more akin to a giant sandbox, a romantic version of the Arabian Nights on American soil. This was more like the bottom of a gravel pit. Disappointing to say the least.

Restless, she reached forward and switched on the radio. Static. She twirled the dial a complete revolution and back again but it was all the same. She twisted around onto her knees and leaned into the back seat looking for a book, a magazine, or maybe a pack of gum, the licorice kind; spearmint gave her a headache.

Her search was in vain. She looked through the rear window before turning back. The shadow of the car stretched far behind them on the pavement. Each rock, stone and tuft of grass was mirrored by a dark twin that elongated before her eyes until it lost all resemblance to its prototype and melted ambiguously into nothingness. All color drained from the landscape.

Gloria was astounded at how quickly day transitions into night in the desert. A glowing sunset, a quick colorful adieu. Nothing remotely resembling a long drawn out dusk. Now you see it, now you don't. Gloria couldn't see a damn thing. Except the glowing red light that indicated the gas tank was empty.

The car rolled over onto the shoulder and stopped.

"Hell's bells," she mumbled and sat there without saying a word.

The "I told you so" hung in the air unsaid. Chloe looked at her mother and then looked out the window into the blackness. Her eyes widened.

"So *this* is night," she thought, startled by the intensity of the blackness. She realized she had never really seen it before. Night had always been hidden by streetlights, car lights, office lights and that peculiar pastel cloud that hung over the Chicago after dark. This was really night. Amazing. Look at the stars. Star light. Star bright.

I'm going to find the little girl's room," said Gloria, opening the door and startling Chloe out of her revelry.

"Watch out for snakes, warned Chloe, remembering reading somewhere that rattle snakes came out at night to lay on the asphalt to keep warm.

"My god!" said Gloria, completely horrified. She instantly retracted her endangered foot and slammed the car door.

Chloe attempted to hide her amusement as the two of them considered the options. In the end Gloria cautiously opened the door and approached it in a very unladylike fashion, her feet never touching the ground. Chloe silently savored her humiliation as she reached into her pocket and passed her mother a Kleenex.

The star-studded night passed with the two huddled together in the back seat of the Bel Aire trying to stay warm. Envisioning a hostile world inhabited by rattlesnakes, tarantulas, scorpions, and Gila monsters gathering around their vehicle in an ever-tightening circle, the two forced the windows tightly closed with an extra twist of the handle and stuffed anklets and lingerie in the vents. Still shivering they fluffed the entire contents of Chloe's suitcase around them and burrowed down in the nest for warmth.

Above them the immeasurable expanse of dazzling constellations danced endlessly across the sky oblivious to all activity in a small, red automobile in the middle of a desert on an insignificant planet in a tiny solar system in of itself inconsequential in the infinite void.

With a burst of sunshine night departed as abruptly as it had arrived. Gloria emerged first from the nest gasping for air and sweating from the heat. Addressing what ever god or devil had created Nevada, she muttered in no uncertain terms that she didn't appreciate the joke.

Remembering the snakes, she scrambled up on the hood of the car. That's when she spotted the semi barreling down upon them. She stood on the car and waved her arms.

Two burly truck drivers, their curiosity clearly piqued, climbed down from the cab.

"You got trouble?" the first grinned and asked.

"We're out of gas," replied Gloria, both relieved and nervous at seeing the two men out in the middle of nowhere. She slid off the hood, lost her balance and fell directly to her knees just as Chloe emerged from the far side of the car.

"Oh please, just let me wake up first," Chloe was thinking as she saw the bigger man help her mother up. "This could go wrong in so many ways."

But her mother seemed to have the situation under control. Even though Jake had just remodeled the interior of the cab with new, red, plush upholstery and a handsome sleeping area behind the seat, Gloria declined the tour of the vehicle. She also turned down Roy's generous offer to climb up for a ride to the Last Chance Gas and Grill they had just passed the day before. She was politely firm on both these points and, since the men were apparently gentlemen in wolves' clothing after all, they offered another plan.

After mustering a generous smile and a wave hello from a distance, Chloe disappeared for a few minutes over the first rise. She reappeared and sat on a rock, sipping yesterday's tepid orange crush. Her stomach was grumbling. She watched as Jake showed her mother his iron cross tattoo while Roy, gold earring glinting in the sun, rolled open the back of the truck to reveal the bulging gas tanks of three Harley Davidsons, each emblazoned with a winged death's head, tucked between the boxes of refrigerators, stoves and other household appliances. "Choppers" the truckers fondly called them.

The first two bikes belonged to Jake and Roy. The third belonged to a friend who had had a little altercation with an East Bay cycle club back in California. He was picking up a little R&R at West Side Memorial while his cast set. They were watching his bike 'til he got out.

"Plenty of gas in these," they grinned, and began to siphon a few gallons for Gloria.

"She really is good," Chloe admitted as she watched the rescue unfold. "You really have to hand it to her sometimes."

She emptied her soda and got back in the car.

When the two vehicles parted the black asphalt was already softening in the sun. Everybody waved enthusiastically. A good time had been had by all.

∞

"Well déjà vu," said Gloria 100 miles later. Ahead was a flashing neon mud flap girl on a bronco riding toward them at 60 mph.

"It's a palindrome," said Chloe.

"A what"

"A palindrome," she repeated. "We did them in fifth grade. Words that are the same backwards and forwards. Like "race car" or "noon". Nevada is like one giant palindrome, exactly the same coming and going."

Chloe was not a laugh out loud kind of little girl but she enjoyed an occasional display of wit when it popped up, especially her own.

After sitting patiently at the pump for a full five minutes Gloria surmised that the concept of a full-service gas station had escaped these people. She climbed out of the car and fumbled with the hoses.

"Give me the money, Mother, I'll go pay," said Chloe.

Gloria walked into the cafe and Chloe went into the station. She paid for the gas and put her mother's change in her left pocket. She put her hand in her right pocket and pulled out her own money.

"I need two gas cans," she told the man behind the candy counter.

He stepped into the back and returned with two red metal containers.

"That'll be two bucks for the containers. It'll cost four eighty to fill them. Be sure you put the nozzle way down in there and hang on or the gas'll go all over."

Chloe handed him the last of her money.

"Thanks," she said and headed back to the car.

Although she had filled the cans as directed they still seemed wet, so she wrapped a loose towel around them before sticking them in the trunk, wedging them firmly between the suitcases. Then she joined her mother for breakfast.

It was mid-afternoon before they stopped again.

"Let's buy something," said Gloria as she approached a big red and white souvenir sign accented with wooden lizards and over-sized tomahawks.

Chloe was hot and crabby and couldn't imagine what she would want here. She could taste the dust lodged in her teeth. Her head ached from the smell of the gasoline that clung to her from their last stop.

Below the tomahawks' feathers a middle-aged man and two little boys sat drinking orange sodas and throwing a stick for a ratty looking underfed little dog. It was the sodas that attracted Chloe's attention.

"Souvenirs." Gloria replied simply.

"Drinks," chimed in Chloe.

They turned off the highway and stopped in front of the hitching post, leaving the car in the shop's borderless parking lot that was indistinguishable from the rest of the landscape. The ten-foot wooden thermometer on the side of the building read ninety-three degrees. It was manually adjusted every two hours by the man in the cowboy hat who sat at its base. He had lost his primary job recently and was left to sit back and practice flipping cigarette butts into a row of cans arranged in a long line going away from him, toward the parking lot. Gloria left her sweater in the car and grabbed only her purse. Together they strode through the heat and dust to the souvenir shop. A man on the front porch greeted them and followed them inside.

The poorly lit store was actually a relief from the hours of sun reflected off sand, gravel and blacktop. Chloe stood in the doorway waiting for her eyes to adjust. She decided that if she bought anything it would be sunglasses.

Gloria bought them a couple of sodas. They took turns using the bathroom and settled comfortably into sipping their drinks and examining the merchandise.

The interior of the shop resembled a miniature Woolworth's, it's items large and small arranged in row upon row of rough, unfinished wooden bins attached to the walls and along narrow aisles. Little birch bark canoes were piled next to tiny kachina dolls. Rubber knives kept company with miniature bows and arrows. Plastic masked men rode rearing stallions. The masks could actually be removed so you could see the face of the man behind it. So far no one had recognized him. There was no rhyme or reason to the choice of nick-knacks the owner thought his customers would consider indigenous to the area.

A display of fine stones, including "genuine" fool's gold, tiger eye agates, and low-grade turquoise, kept company with a variety of small rocks which in all likelihood were gathered just off the front porch and were personally polished by the proprietor himself. The finer specimens, like the rose quartz and the petrified coral, were each glued to a thin piece of white cardboard printed with a description of the stone and its place of origin: Kuala Lumpur; northern Siberia; Grand Forks, North Dakota.

The more expensive items were pretty much the same as the plastic and rubber ones except that they were made of "hand blown glass" or "genuine leather" and lived on the shelves along the wall at about eye level. The shelves were interrupted periodically by small windows hollowed out of the adobe colored stucco walls.

Gloria and Chloe strolled quietly along together in the heat looking at a row of green glass iguanas with dots of red glass for eyes. Just as they came to the window an enormous explosion caused the entire shop to shake uncontrollably and a full row of little glass horses galloped right off the top shelf and shattered on the floor.

Gloria and Chloe watched as their car, framed by the small, glassless window, disappeared in a mass of billowing smoke and flames. Both Gloria and Chloe stared blankly ahead at the window as if it were an animated painting hanging on the wall. A small handful of dogs and children ran into the painting from some previously nonexistent dimension and circled the fire excitedly. Two men came out of the truck stop in the background and watched enthusiastically. No sirens shrieked. No fire trucks raced to the scene.

The proprietor abandoned his clients and left his shop to enjoy the spectacle. There was a long break in their conversation while Gloria and Chloe stared at the ball of flames. Gloria broke the silence.

"The red ones or the green ones?" Gloria asked her daughter holding up two pairs of sunglasses.

"The green, I think," said her daughter.

Gloria kept the red and handed Chloe the green.

They donned their glasses, set their money on the counter and left by the back door.

16
DON'T STOP NOW

Gloria, true to her nature, never looked back. Chloe, on the other hand, could not resist turning just one time to view the barren landscape accented by the adobe shop. She could see right in the back door, through the shop and out the little window to the disaster beyond. Black smoke hung in the air. The little western diorama remained seared into her brain for months to come. Guilt tends to lend permanence to events better forgotten.

After about half an hour of standing by the road wishing Jake and Roy or anyone comparable would show up in a truck with a comfy remodel in the back and respond to their thumbs in the air, Gloria sat down in the dirt and began to sob.

"I want to go home," she cried. Tears would have been streaming down her cheeks had they not evaporated instantly in the moisture-less air.

"What was I thinking?" she blubbered forlornly. "We're going to die here. I want to go home."

Chloe was feeling increasingly bleak herself and not as willing to parent her mother as she had been at other times. She wanted her mother to shut up and leave her to wait patiently for rescue while she remained focused on one of her usual mantras. She was losing the struggle to control her own panic. "Into the Valley of Death …into the Valley of Death …," she chanted, unable to come up with the next line. Her optimism and focus had evaporated with her mother's tears.

It was not without considerable effort that she reached deep inside herself and found Kammel setting out with his twenty men. She envisioned herself being pulled up behind him and galloping off into the sunset leaving her mother behind.

This was her way. She didn't know the Lord's pray.

"We can't go back," she said simply. "We have no home. You sold the house."

She was kind enough not to add, "We have no friends. You have no job. You have no husband to care for us. I'm not enrolled in school. We are outcasts and our reputations, for whatever reasons, cannot be repaired." Her mind raced on in that vein.

She was frantically trying to beat down the thought of the gas cans she had hidden in the trunk and the roll they must have played in their demise.

She added simply, "we hated it there anyway."

It was the best she could do under the circumstances.

Above them circled three large vultures who drooled down at them whispering "nevermore". Chloe stared up at them wondering if there was a DNA link that allowed vultures and ravens to speak the same language or if large carnivorous birds were schooled jointly in the airways as they migrated where ever it is they migrate to. Where ever it was she wished these three would go there now.

"Get up. Here comes a car." She announced. This car had to be the one to take them. She too felt terrible in every way and wondered seriously if they might in fact die here in the desert.

Gloria rose and presented herself to the oncoming car in her best model on the runway pose, which she pulled off astoundingly well under the circumstances. Chloe stood to her mother's right and slightly to the rear. (It was a slight adjustment to the forward position to which she had been trained since infancy.) She waved a red scarf in the air, level with Gloria's head, knowing this would attract the driver's attention and at the same time accentuate Gloria's sparkling blonde hair. It was Pavlovian. She couldn't help herself.

The Rambler pulled up next to them without hesitation. The man riding shotgun stuck his head out a little farther.

"Hi," he grinned. "Hop in" he said, without bothering to ask where Gloria and Chloe were going. There were, after all, only two directions out here. This way and that way. If she weren't standing on this side of the highway going this way she would be on the other side of the highway going that way. That's all there was to it.

A quick glance told Chloe these two guys looked moderately normal. She ignored the little whining inner voice warning her of the anonymity of mass murderers. This seemed to be their first and last hope of rescue and she had no intention of passing it up. She immediately took control of the situation.

"Thanks," she said cheerfully, as if she did this sort of thing every day. She pushed her mother into the back seat, attempting to block the view of Gloria's red swollen eyes and defeated demeanor at least until the door clicked shut behind them.

She slipped Gloria the Kleenex which she always carried in her pocket.

In retrospect Chloe may have sat back down in the dust and waited however long necessary for the next car, but of course hind sight is always perfect. How was she to know?

After brief introductions that were a pack of lies all the way around, the foursome cruised lightheartedly down the highway. The breeze from the open windows fanned them mercifully. Both Gloria and Chloe fled into the emotional refuge of a dead sleep about ten minutes into the drive. When Chloe awoke she stared silently out the window counting miler markers. A small highway identification sign reared its ugly head. "93" it said. She jabbed her mother hard in the ribs and Gloria came to abruptly.

"We're on the wrong road!" Chloe whispered frantically in her mother's ear. "50! 50! It's supposed to say 50! We're going the wrong way! Where are they taking us?!"

The man riding shot gun, as attractive and mild mannered as he had appeared in his plaid flannel shirt with the sleeves rolled up and the errant lock of hair hanging down to the black lenses of his silver sun glasses, was revealing himself to be a weird and scary sort of guy. He was, generally speaking, a maniac of the first degree. He rambled on about politics and boar hunting while he drank whiskey and waved his .44 Magnum out the window. (He and the Nebraskan policeman shared the opinion that, although the Colt 45 was a useful sidearm, the .44 Magnum was by far the most powerful round.) Occasionally he blasted away at an unsuspecting jack rabbit or prairie dog and even in his inebriated state managed to annihilate one or two.

"He hardly ever shoots people," his friend the driver assured them brightly, "but if I were you I'd lay low back there for a while."

Chloe immediately shrank out of sight but Gloria had questions.

"Where are we going?" was the first.

"Las Vegas! Las Vegas, my dear!" was the enthusiastic response.

"But *we* are not going to Las Vegas."

"But *we* are going to Las Vegas."

"Not us."

"Well us are."

"Well us are not!" stated Gloria firmly.

They bantered back and forth in a sort of call and response fashion reminiscent of Southern religious rallies until the sound of their voices was overwhelmed by the babbling of the driver's companion.

"Sniveling vermin. Odorous pile of putrefied, stinking rot." shouted the gun wielding psychopath. Whether he was addressing the rodents fleeing across the parched terrain or the politicians whose names spewed from his mouth was unclear.

"We can drop you off here," offered the driver," but we're not going back."

"Where is here," Gloria asked reluctantly.

"About an hour south of Ely. Fascinating little burg. Smattering of people, a couple of diners, handful of houses and a bus depot. You may like the later. But you'd have to tell them where it is you want to go before you buy a ticket."

"And you'd drop us off right here?" asked Gloria looking out the window incredulously and recalling the near-death experience on the roadside a few hours earlier.

"Right here," came the reply.

"How far is Las Vegas?" she asked next.

"200 miles, give or take a few."

"Do they have a bus depot?"

"Hell, they have an airport and sure, an excellent bus depot, too."

"Then Las Vegas it is," said Gloria.

"Here we come Las Vegas," grinned the driver.

Chloe was mortified. She was speechless. Well, she was usually speechless but this time she couldn't even find the words to speak to herself.

"Close the windows, would you?" asked the driver politely as he closed his own and lit a cigarette. He passed it back to Chloe's mother. She said she didn't smoke and he laughed again. He was as giddy as his friend was pugnacious. Gloria laughed too. Soon they were all laughing, even Chloe, who didn't find any of this funny in the least and wished someone would open the windows again, it was getting too smoky to breath in here.

A bag of potato chips and half a bag of caramel candy was rapidly devoured between the lot of them. The psychopath was mumbling unintelligibly except for a few shouts of "Viva Las Vegas", "Viva Zapata", and "Viva Sonny Liston", followed by "drive, jefe, drive" and "una mas cervesa por favor". Then he fell silent.

The driver had also decided to clear his throat with a couple of beers. Gloria, not a fan of drunk driving, objected to the later and offered to drive. Chloe clutched her mother's knee in a panic and refused to sit in the back alone with either of these sleaze bags.

"Chloe will drive," announced her mother.

"Balls, woman, she can't drive," responded the driver, now on the threshold of serious inebriation. "She's not old enough."

"Of course, she is. She's older than you think."

He pulled over and changed places with Chloe. As he passed her he gave her a brief sympathetic look and said, "I'll bet you are."

He slid in the back and pulled his hat over his eyes. Just stay on 93. It's 93 all the way. They were all asleep before Chloe had the car out of park.

Chloe took a few minutes to familiarize herself with the Rambler. Wipers, lights, radio, .44 magnum.

She slipped her thumb and forefinger around the handle and slid the gun out of Senor Psychopath's hand and under her seat. With that taken care of she yanked the gears into drive and swung onto the highway. She swung a little more than anyone noticed and stuck to 93…. going north.

About an hour later she quietly pulled into an empty parking lot and stopped the car. Slowly and noiselessly she opened the door.

Carefully she awakened her mother and extricated her from the snoring mass.

A few minutes later they both fell breathlessly into adjoining seats of the greyhound bus which was waiting on the other side of the block at the Ely bus depot.

Part II
CROSSROADS

17

WE'RE HEEERE

Gloria and Chloe sat in the window of their room on the tenth floor of the St. Francis Hotel looking out at the city of San Francisco, the Bay, the Golden Gate Bridge and the morning mist engulfing it all. When they tumbled groggily from the bus the night before they hailed a cab on Folsom Street and told the driver to take them to "a nice hotel". He pushed those instructions to the limit, Gloria succumbed to the temptation and here they were.

"My God," she whispered, "we're in San Francisco! Now what? The view really is stupendous. Oh my God! What am I doing here?"

She leaned back into the armchair by the window, dug her toes into the incredible cashmere blanket that lay across her lap, and loosened the towel from around her head. Her newly washed hair tumbled to her shoulders. She inhaled the smell of shampoo. She loved the smell of shampoo.

She also loved the smell of clean sheets, especially when she had nothing to do with cleaning them. She loved the feather pillow under her head. She loved the way the crystal tear drops hanging from the chandelier above her cast little rainbows across the outline of her body under the soft layer of blankets. Even with her eyes shut she could feel the colors playing across her contours. She loved the rich heavy curtains that fell from ceiling to floor on either side of the windows and the flimsy, billowy fabric that hung across the glass, softly filtering the light. She loved the vase of ferns and lilies. She loved the little pieces of linen left on the floor near the bed so her bare feet would never touch the floor and she absolutely adored calling out "later please" in a tinkling aristocratic voice when the maid came to the door to make up the room. It was almost more than she could bear. For these reasons she had lain in bed feigning sleep for nearly an hour after she first opened her eyes.

Gloria drifted back to sleep and was awakened by Chloe coming in the door. She tried again to recapture her previous blissful state but it dawned on her that the only thing in the room that wasn't perfect and pristine was her. She slid out of bed and into the shower.

When she finally felt equal to her surroundings, Gloria slipped from the shower and into the armchair near the window where she now sat. She gazed dreamily into the mist.

"Now what," kept ricocheting through her mind. The phrase careened in and out of her consciousness at an annoying speed leaving little jet trails that clouded her general air of success and contentment. They dissipated rapidly but left little puffs of insecurity in their wake.

Her wish had come true. Here she was. Now what? She felt like celebrating and mourning at the same time. This was the day after The Arrival. The show was over. Sometime in the night the programs had been crumpled and discarded and the cleaning crew had appeared and swept everything in the trash. She was triumphant yet in her heart there was a certain inexplicable hint of emptiness. The emptiness was crisscrossed with the jet trails and the puffy little clouds. Among the clouds flashed a whimsical billboard that read 'That's All Folks' with a little Disney Hanna-Barbera copyright mark in the lower right corner.

"Let's eat" piped up Chloe and the whole scenario disappeared. They dug enthusiastically into the breakfast that room service had elaborately provided. Gloria had never paid for room service before, or for hotels for that matter. Thinking back at all the hotels and room service she had used in the past and not personally paid for she suddenly had an increased appreciation of the many benefits of being well dressed. She decided that once she had gotten acclimated she really needed to go shopping. She could not afford not to. She dressed once more in the only clothes she had that were not a pile of ashes.

Chloe, for once, could not contain her excitement. "It's so beautiful!" she exclaimed as she gazed out the window, English muffin in one hand and honey dripping off the knife she was waving in the other. Chloe was actually verging on chatty.

"Look, look, the fog is moving away. I can see the bridge. The Golden Gate Bridge! I can actually see it. This is the best idea you ever had! This is going to be great!"

She stuffed the last of the muffin in her mouth and buttered another.

"Look, down there, there's a park. We're up on a hill. Wow, it's really steep."

The reserved and practical Chloe had apparently been left on the bus or some where on the desert floor. Wherever she was, this Chloe didn't miss her.

She launched into a detailed monologue describing her foray through the halls while her mother had slept. She described the decorations in the hotel hallways, including the pattern on the carpet, the design on the wallpaper and the maids pushing carts from room to room. She had greeted an elegant elderly woman who had smiled back oddly at Chloe in her dirty, crop-top shirt and grungy shorts and tennis shoes. She had seen a freshly showered, young couple on their way to breakfast. They had failed to acknowledge Chloe at all. Chloe looked down at her own dusty, well-travel ensemble and hoped she met no other guests until she bought a change of clothes.

"What on earth has gotten into you?" exclaimed Gloria. "I've never seen you like this."

"And without note cards," she wanted to add, but tactfully did not. Gloria was not completely oblivious to Chloe's conversational struggles.

Chloe had never stayed in a hotel before and, although she had spent a great deal of time riding an escalator in Chicago, until the previous evening, she had never ridden in an elevator either. When she stepped inside the one waiting at the end of the hall she was too intimidated by the bell boy to direct him to take her to the lobby. Embarrassed, she stepped out again and glanced impatiently down the hallway as if waiting for a companion who was apparently taking too long brushing her teeth. Eventually the elevator was called to another floor. She ran down the stairs to the ninth floor; strolled nonchalantly down the hall; ran again down the stairs at the opposite end of the building to the eighth floor; changed direction once more and climbed the stairs back to the tenth. She peered out the windows at the end of each hall, in an attempt to catch a glimpse of her new hometown.

Gloria listened absentmindedly to Chloe while watching the Golden Gate Bridge appear and disappear repeatedly among the rolling clouds. The view really was incredible. Boats on the bay dissolved in the swirling mist then materialized somewhere else. The water itself was indistinguishable from the fog, giving the small crafts a fascinating airborne quality. The morning sun found its way through openings in the shifting mist and made every dewy surface sparkle.

"Let's stay for a week at least," begged Chloe.

Gloria gave in to the temptation to smile broadly and poured herself some coffee.

"Two days," she said. "We can do this for two days. Then, we have to move into our own place. One day to see the town. One day to find an apartment. That's the way it has to be."

Beneath Gloria's flashy exterior and sizable bank account lived a frugal woman. For most of her life there had been no other option. She had recently justified the expense of her wardrobe because of the obvious benefits, making them, in her estimation, practical clothing. However, even Gloria knew she could not survive on clothes alone.

Gloria was acutely aware that for both social and financial reasons some type of substantial income would soon be required. Even with the church money, retiring at twenty-nine was not a practical course of action. In addition, she did not want her relationships with men to be misconstrued. Men were a diversion, a pastime, a hobby and, yes, a necessity in some ways, but she absolutely would not cross the line and consider them employment, regardless of what some of those stifled women back in Elmwood might have said. Gloria had always been aware that when men lavish money and gifts on wealthy women it is all very 'chi-chi', and part of the game. When men do the same for poor women it is called something entirely different. Gloria needed a real job so that she could continue to accept money and gifts from men without tarnishing her sterling reputation. Retirement would have to wait.

She gave up trying to comb her hair dry. In this weather it simply wasn't going to happen. She pinned her loose curls up in a fashion reminiscent of Grace Kelly in her last Hitchcock movie. Gloria loved that movie. She glanced at the mirror over the bureau across the room. Her wet hair looked less like the Princess's than she had hoped. She quickly wrapped the scarf from her waist around her head giving her a flare more reminiscent of Lauren Bacall than of the Princess of Monaco. She glanced in the mirror again. Lauren was good.

She leaned back in her chair and exhaled deeply. The fog was burning off and her gaze reached all the way to a pretty little island out on the bay. She wondered vaguely who lived out there? Was it a high rent district? Was the shopping good? In a round about way she began thinking about money again. Gloria was in no financial panic but she was becoming uncomfortably alert. The coffee was pushing her alertness to the border of agitation. She and Chloe had slept in until 10:00 am and they both felt refreshed and relaxed in the way one only feels after surviving a brush with death, real or simply imagined. Unfortunately, a good night's sleep sometimes clears the head just enough to recognize the mess you are in. Gloria had used up all her emotional and intellectual resources on breaking out of the Midwest. Now she looked out on the Bay Area without an inkling of what to do next. The vague notion of finding an apartment and getting a job carried about as much substance as the morning mist. Gloria's smile faded slightly. She needed a diversion, a nice drive. She thought of her flaming car and began biting her nails, an activity very unlike her. She looked out at San Francisco, waiting all around her, yet so inaccessible.

Her ears began to ring. She shook her head thinking it was a result of the shower. It didn't help. Real bells were clanging outside her head. She looked down at the street below. A cable car was climbing Nob Hill toward her.

"Breakfast is over Chloe. Let's go."

Chloe had also been looking out the window. She knew exactly what her mother was thinking. She snatched up her sweater and beat her mother to the door.

18

LIFELINE

By the time they reached the street below anticipation had replaced introspection. Gloria and Chloe stood side by side and watched eagerly as the heavy, red and gold beast lumbered up the hill swallowing the shiny, wet, steel rails as it went. Gloria was in no hurry to risk being crippled for the sake cheap and amusing transportation. This initial cable car, she insisted, was the observation car and not to be approached. It stopped in the middle of the intersection of California and Taylor. People boarded it en masse from both sides. The conductor released the grip and off they went.

Gloria and Chloe conferred. Pretty straight forward, they agreed, as long as you didn't slip. This was something to be considered, since a light drizzle had just replaced the morning fog. Standing there in the soggy, matted, autumn leaves listening to the automobiles splash past Gloria briefly wondered what had happened to sunny California. A bout of unusual weather, she naively concluded. A second cable car was approaching.

Chloe looked up at her mother.

"This one?" she asked.

"Yes," her mother answered simply, her eyes fixed on the oncoming monster.

It halted with a loud creak and Chloe hopped up the step. She turned and offered her mother a hand. Gloria quickly sat down while Chloe remained standing on the top step, cautiously clinging firmly to a nearby pole. The conductor collected a handful of change from the passengers, released the grip and the beast jerked forward again, continuing its breakfast of metal and mud.

The morning rush hour was nearly over and the car was sparsely filled. It was headed for the financial district down by the Bay Bridge. Higher echelon business people generally drove their own cars or were chauffeured to their offices atop sky scrapers, but the hourly workers were not above a late ride on the California line. A receptionist smoothed her skirt behind her knees with her soft, gloved hand to protect her nylon stockings from snagging on the rough, varnished, wooden benches. A pair of young women, apparently in the typing pool, chatted casually about their boss's mood swings. The man in the singled breasted, wool tweed suit with narrow notched lapels and narrow trousers clung tightly to his leather brief case with one hand and stood upright, grasping a pole with the other. A group of early bird tourists were scattered among the bunch, pointing, grinning and taking pictures as they went.

They crested the hill and, with a "wheeeee ..." from the tourist population, dipped down the other side. Their descent was exciting but brief. When the car stopped at Grant Avenue, Chloe grabbed her mother's sleeve.

"Here," she commanded and before Gloria could protest Chloe yanked her out of her seat and into the intersection. After dodging a few cars, they safely reached the sidewalk. Chloe dropped her mother's arm and walked slowly up to the nearest storefront. Its exotic Asian decor and its large display windows had beckoned her.

In the window stood a large glass urn that was nearly as tall as Chloe was. Wide-eyed and innocently Chloe approached the window trying to discern the contents of the jar. A look of horror spread across her face. In the urn, twisted and squashed to fit, was a fawn, a little baby deer. Chloe gasped, her wide eyes getting wider still.

Carefully positioned around the main attraction were a bevy of other jars and urns containing a variety of other pickled creatures and pickled creature parts. For a moment Chloe held her breath, then she whistled a long Midwestern "ishshsh". China Town would prove full of surprises!

Gloria inhaled sharply and they both backed slowly away. There was nothing more to be said. Nowhere in either of their mental archives was an adequate explanation for what they had just seen. As they walked down the street and past the open door, they could see a long wall covered with small drawers and dark cubbies. An old Asian man measured the contents of one of the apothecary drawers onto a scale, then into a small brown bag. A small woman with jet black hair trailing down her back waited patiently for her purchase. Gloria and Chloe stepped closer to each other and continued walking.

The next shop, to their relief, contained no dead animals that should never have wandered from their roles in Walt Disney specials. Brightly colored silks and faux silks were offered pre-wrapped in plastic bags for easy purchase. The set-up was vaguely reminiscent of the adobe souvenir shop they had fled only yesterday. (Could it be only yesterday?) In Chinatown the wooden bins were not filled with tomahawks and canoes but with pajamas, robes, high-necked blouses fastened with frogs and calf-length pants with zippers up the side. Unlike the items in the adobe shop, Chloe found everything in this store both beautiful and intriguing. She unwrapped a child's little red robe and a pair of little children's slippers. Unable to get them back in the bag she laid them over the rest of the packages in the shape of a little boy. She paused for a moment. She remembered when Hal had been that size. She turned and walked down the isle. In the dim recesses of the shop Chloe spotted a robe mounted on the wall. She walked back and stood looking up at it. It was stunning.

"That one's not for sale," said the saleswoman with an accent Chloe had only heard on late night television. "That was my grandmother's. It is real silk and hand embroidered."

Chloe's fascination was obvious. The girl drew her nearer the robe.

"See the peonies?" she asked. "Peonies are for long life. Very important Chinese symbol."

She took Chloe's hand and traced the embroidery with her fingers.

"It's all embroidered by hand," she repeated. "Silk thread. See the little butterflies?"

At this point Gloria joined them and listened carefully.

"But the bats," the girl continued, indicating the strange shapes between the peonies, "the bats are made with gold thread. There are five little bats on each sleeve. They stand for health, long life, prosperity, virtue, and a peaceful death. See how they fly around the prosperity symbol?"

With her graceful fingers she pointed out a beautiful little circular design.

"My grandmother," the girl added dutifully, "was a happy woman who led a virtuous life. I light incense for her every day."

Gloria only remembered seeing one bat in her life. She had found the furry, wicked-looking, little flying rodent in her shoe one morning and emptied it out the backdoor in disgust. She had no idea how it had gotten in the house. She questioned the artistic abilities of the Chinese. Bats looked nothing like that.

Chloe, however, had seen plenty of bats while lying on her back in the yard after the sun went down. Their black silhouettes had gracefully glided and swooped from tree to tree against the fading light of the night sky. Yes, she thought, bats, of course.

The sales girl recognized a captive audience when she saw one.

"In Chinese the word for bat is 'fu', " she recited knowledgeably. "The word for happiness is also 'fu'."

Her work here was done. It was not difficult after that to sell Chloe a small, rayon scarf with bats and prosperity symbols drifting about in the folds. They left with two pairs of black capris for Gloria and two blue pairs for Chloe. Gloria would have bought almost anything to get them out of their white shorts before they disintegrated off their bodies.

Further down the street they discovered the open store front of a meat market. Featherless chickens and furless rabbits hung outside. Inside lay piles of fish on mounds of ice; each fish staring up vacantly with its single, visible pink eye. Chloe thought of National Geographic photos of strange markets in faraway places. Her fascination overcame her revulsion and she stood mesmerized by the sight while around her people came and went from the store as if this were a perfectly ordinary place.

Gloria also stood mesmerized. In her mind she stood on the corner of Halsted and Ashland Avenue inhaling the scent of Chicago's stockyards. She felt small and helpless, a child again. Smell and memory. A waft of ginger and five spice powder revived her and she pulled Chloe down the street to where the contents of a busy corner dry goods store spilled colorfully out onto the sidewalk in all directions. Colorful streamers blew in the breeze. Fancy, paper dragons with sparkling, flowing manes caught every small gust of wind. Inside the store the two found a variety of snacks including candies with edible wrappers and salty, dried cuttlefish in cellophane bags.

Chloe could have spent days in this amazing world of San Francisco's Chinatown. Gloria, on the other hand, had begun to glance repeatedly over her shoulder, trying to keep sight of the cable car, her lifeline to the St. Francis.

Chloe saw her mother looking lost and unsteady.

"Let's cross the street and go back," she suggested, remembering her mother crying in the dust only the day before.

The two stepped off the curb and retraced their route on the sunny side of the street. They glanced at displays of jewelry and jade, Buddhas and temple dogs, but they spent most of their time looking at people. There was no way getting around the fact that the majority of these people were not from the Midwest. Their parents and grandparents had not sprung from the loins of Puritans, Pilgrims, and Quakers. They did not arrive as a result of the Great Potato Famine. There was nary a Viking among them and none of them could possibly be named "Vlad".

Gloria cocked her head slightly and astutely surmised that "these people" must use an entirely different line of makeup. How did they all manage to keep their hair so uniformly black? That blue tinge could not be natural, maybe it was some kind of highlighting you could get at a beauty salon. She looked at her reflection in a window and wondered how that blue highlight would look on her own blonde hair.

The cable line passed by a bakery. When they reached it the car was nowhere in sight. They stepped in and purchased a couple of delicious looking pastries with yellow icing. The car rumbled down the hill and stopped to allow Chloe and Gloria to seat themselves for the ride downhill. Chloe and Gloria took out their treats, anticipating the melt-in-the mouth sweetness. Their teeth sank through the bread into the ball of lard in the middle.

"That's darn tasty," said Gloria, "but I think I'm full."

"I'm full, too," said Chloe.

"Have some gum, I've spearmint in my bag," offered Gloria.

The two chewed vigorously for the next few minutes as they descended the east side of Nob Hill. Their view of the East Bay disappeared as they entered the realm of dark, hulking skyscrapers that flourished nowhere else in San Francisco. The financial district loomed above them on all sides.

Gloria twisted and strained in search of windows full of jewelry, dresses or shoes.

Her efforts were in vain.

"Not much to buy here," Gloria commented, seriously missing the big picture. Let's just ride through and get out of the dark. I'll bet the sun never touches the ground down here. Besides, I'm getting hungry. The gum wasn't very filling.

"I'm hungry, too. Next time I'd like two pieces, please," requested Chloe.

Up the hill they went, out of the land of darkness and big business and into the land of sun and light. The rain had stopped, the fog had burned off and the day was beautiful.

19
POLK STREET

The St. Francis rose up in front of them, then disappeared behind them as Gloria and Chloe rolled down the west side of Nob Hill. At the last moment, the two had chosen not to abandon their adventures for the safety of lunch at the hotel. Instead, they continued down the hill, past the park and onward toward what Chloe would later learn was Grace Cathedral, the most awesome cathedral Chloe had seen since that time in Chicago when her mother had nearly gone home with the little man behind the curly, black mustache.

Chloe's blood ran cold.

"No, no, no," she prayed silently as the monumental edifice came into view.

"Yes, yes, yes," thought Gloria, gleefully shouting internal "hosannas" as she made a mental note of its exact size and location. She had hoped that the religious chapter of her life was over but under the circumstances a second reading might be useful.

Gloria's heart opened again to the lord and her soul began to glow. With a renewed sense of purpose, she lightheartedly announced that they would disembark on Polk Street, which appeared to have some kind of festive air about it even though this was only a Wednesday, and noon to boot. Wondering if they had forgotten a holiday, Chloe and Gloria walked along delighted to have relocated to such a convivial city.

They passed a number of men holding hands and chatting. Chloe pointed out two cheerful young guys walking along with their hands in each others back pockets. Chloe, being younger and considerably more naive, thought California was a really friendly and special place. And it was.

Gloria thought about it for a few minutes and weighed the evidence in light of a more adult perspective before coming to the same decision. In the end she was even more delighted than Chloe was. She had noticed a number of things Chloe hadn't; no one had harassed her on the street; no one intentionally brushed intimately against her body; and although she had heard a few cat calls, none of them had been directed toward her. What a great place. She would date elsewhere, she would shop elsewhere, she might even work elsewhere but this neighborhood she intended to call home.

They sat in a booth in the window of a Polk Street restaurant and ordered ham sandwiches and sodas. Gloria asked the waiter for a newspaper, she had seen a rack as they had come in. She spread the want adds across the table in front of them.

Once again Gloria bemoaned the loss of her beloved Bel Aire. Without a car the housing prospects were severely limited and besides, Gloria couldn't help remembering how good she had looked behind the wheel. Chloe shrank a little lower in her seat and gazed out the window.

They compared the ads in the paper to a map of the California Street cable car route Gloria sketched from memory on the back of a napkin. The options narrowed. An apartment on California Street anywhere from Polk to Taylor would keep them mobile and in the neighborhood. A block leeway on ether side might be acceptable, but that was unexplored territory. Who knew what might be out there.

The napkin representation was frustrating. Gloria's memory was not that good. She motioned to a waiter and asked for a better map. He pulled one from the rack near the front door and handed it to her. The map fell open and a whole new concept of the city exploded before her. It was a bit like Magellan letting Spain drop off the edge of the earth and finding himself still afloat.

At first it was exhilarating. There was a world beyond the two block strip that bordered the California line. There were even two more cable car routes. Then fear set in. Good lord there were streets and blocks and neighborhoods and parks and bus lines everywhere. San Francisco was huge. This looked liked Chicago. Gloria's head whirled deliriously at what she saw. Then, after a few moments of intense vertigo, she recoiled in denial and clung to her previously limited understanding of the city. It was better that way. This was too much too soon. She gasped for breath, yanked her eyes upward and looked desperately out the window for reassurance. A slow exhale of relief followed. This was obviously not Chicago.

Chicago was like a different planet. The buildings were different. The people were clearly different in every way. Everything here seemed cleaner. There were hills downtown and the air smelled like the ocean. She hadn't seen the ocean yet but she could already taste it on the air. She had only been here one day and this much was already clear.

"One neighborhood at a time, one neighborhood at a time ..." she whispered to no one in particular.

They finished their lists and their sandwiches and departed taking the blasphemous map with them. They hopped the next car going their way, albeit a little less vigorously than they had earlier. Food, responsibility, and the general noise and activity of the city were beginning to weigh them both down.

Chloe sunk silently onto the wooden bench. Now that the ham sandwich had absorbed her adrenaline her optimism wavered. She stared openly at the jumble of people all around her and knew, even at her age, that there was a social pyramid involving them all. She also knew that it would only take a nudge to plummet them to the bottom of it. Only her mother stood between her and disaster. It wasn't a particularly comforting thought.

Chloe tried to imagine what she might do if Gloria sat down and cried on the corner of California and Hyde the way she had in the sands of Nevada. What if something worse happened? She didn't know any doctors here and she didn't know how to get to a department store for emergency shopping therapy. She had to watch carefully for the signs and not let her mother get too tired or let her feel too forlorn.

Then there was the whole love and affection issue; a surprising and relatively new turn of events. When Gloria found another boyfriend or had another breakdown where would Chloe be this time? When Gloria became bored with Chloe, where was the rooftop she could run to? Where was the attic she could climb to?

Chloe stared ahead, tired and glassy-eyed, as they headed back to the hotel. The cable car stopped and two more couples piled on.

"Kammel was out with twenty men," Chloe began her mantra but her weary mind searched vainly for the next verse. She was really in need of a nap.

The car lurched up the hill.

Now Chloe was not looking at the afternoon sun reflecting off the pastel buildings or at the cool, green shade of Huntington Park. This time she saw the man sleeping on the stoop of a cheap apartment building and the tired, worn, old women pushing a shopping cart up the hill.

The rumble of the cable car was not loud enough to drown out her thoughts. Chloe had felt safer in the desert surrounded by snakes than in the city with only her mother for protection.

Then a most surprising thing happened. When the cable car stopped at California and Taylor, Gloria got off first, turned, and offered Chloe her hand. Chloe took it and together they walked into the hotel. Still holding hands, they entered the elevator. Chloe looked at her reflection in the mirrored walls, hand in hand with her mother. Silently she thanked the boys on Polk Street for setting the example.

20

HOME SWEET HOME

In the end, it had not taken one day to find an apartment but four. It would have taken infinitely longer had Chloe not taken matters into her own hands. Gloria stood by her decision to vacate the Mark Hopkins after two nights. They packed their meager belongings neatly into their Jade Heaven shopping bags. Gloria put on her make-up. Chloe glanced sideways into the mirror at her mother and recognized that, even without make-up, her mother was looking better and better all the time. They exited as they always had, with Chloe in formation slightly front and right, in case anyone significant might spot them. As they descended the steps, Gloria noticed that her choreography was outdated. Chloe was no longer just hiding Gloria's hips but upstaging her altogether. The truth evoked no hard feelings. In fact, she felt a certain amount of admiration for her creation. Nevertheless, she intended to spend some time re-staging upcoming departures.

They walked as far as the upper edge of the Tenderloin. It was a profoundly short walk. Just a few blocks downhill from the most prestigious neighborhood in town was the old red light district. The name was left over from the 1930s when this vice riddled neighborhood was well known for alleged police corruption. It was said that the local officers took so many bribes that they could afford the best cuts of beef.

The desk man at the first hotel they entered offered to pass them clean linens through an opening in a twisted grate as he offered them the hourly rates. They fled. The hotel they finally moved into was not much better, but it was cheap, said Gloria, and they would only be there one night.

Girl's giggled, men bellowed, doors slammed and bed's rocked. After just one sleepless night Chloe's desire to find an apartment increased exponentially. By the second morning it had soared into infinity. Oddly enough, Gloria's ability to function plummeted with every passing hour. Her refusal to spend money was crippling her. They could not leave California Street because Gloria had no car. She couldn't buy a car because she had no money. She couldn't get a job until she had a place to live. Without a job she wouldn't have the money to buy a car. Ignoring the fact that at this particular moment she possessed a very plump investment portfolio from her ex, the money from the sale of the house, and what was left of the lawsuit with the church, Gloria pictured herself wasting away in a hotel like this very one without a penny to her name. A complete captive of her own black logic, Gloria was too depressed to step out of bed. She just slept and cried.

After the second night of short naps and shorter dreams Chloe awoke tired but optimistic. Her mother's tears barely phased her.

"A day of crying a breakdown doth not make," she reminded herself.

She picked up an orange soda to go with her peanut butter sandwich and walked up to Huntington Park to enjoy breakfast in the grass. She knew her mother was just flushing the negativity and frustration from her system.

"Everybody deserves to enjoy a good cry now and then," she told herself. She herself had not done so in about six years but apparently other people did it and it was considered perfectly normal. This was not "The Big One" she told the bats as she unfolded her scarf and lay it before her on the grass. Earlier, when she had slipped the scarf into her pocket, she had wondered briefly if it would ruin her line, but the beautiful little bats told her not to worry. The scarf was silky and lightweight, they said, and line wasn't everything. Their conversation was a little high-pitched but Chloe got the general idea.

She was now prepared to go apartment hunting. She knew it was up to her. She had forged the signature on a deposit check earlier so it would appear as if her mother had actually signed it.

Chloe dressed in her new Chinese capris, blue tennis shoes and her only shirt, the white midi one. Time to pound the pavement. At 89 pounds the pounding was light but pounding nevertheless. She abandoned her want ads in the park and walked door to door craning her neck to catch a glimpse of any elusive for rent signs hung on a door knob or tucked in a front window. She was methodical and persistent by nature. She was polite, talkative and straightforward out of desperation.

Chloe walked towards the top of California Street and circled the park above Grace Cathedral. She explained to the first landlady her need for accommodations for herself and her mother, who was ill at the moment and resting in their room at the Belvedere Hotel. The woman told her to put her check back in her pocket, sat her down in the sitting room with a cookie, and promptly called social services. Chloe heard the conversation, liberated a few more cookies and slipped out the door.

After that her check stayed in her pocket and her mother was not sick but across the street looking at another place. No matter. This block was way too expensive. Apparently the price of lodging was inversely related to the distance from the St. Francis and she needed to go downhill. Somewhere between Jones and Leavenworth she found a place she could afford but noticed the sticker from the fumigation company on the window. It had monthly dates on it indicating regular visits. Chloe was disgusted.

Towards the bottom of the hill, some where around Hyde Street, she inadvertently gave the impression that she and her mother were looking for a place from which to do business together. The landlord was interested in calling the police. Apparently the name of her present accommodations needed to be left entirely out of the conversation.

She crossed the street and started back up the hill. From this perspective the world was primarily concrete. The trees grew at a 45-degree angle to the side walk. Going down the hill she had been able to see for blocks, she felt airy and lighthearted every time she took a step. She had seen people, sky and little dwarf trees pruned to fit the city space. The trees reached up with their little pruned fists greeting birds and airplanes. It was uplifting. Now she looked down at her feet so she wouldn't trip over them as she trudged upward. From this angle she noticed the different grades of gravel in the sidewalk, the occasional candy wrappers and intermittent cigarette butts. As her feet climbed her heart sank. She sat down on the stoop of a soft-green apartment with faded white columns at the top of the steps.

The concrete was cold even though she was on the sunny side of the street. It was almost noon but the fog had only just burned off. San Francisco was still chilly and dank. She had forgotten her sweater. She heard the door slam behind her and she turned to see a woman coming down the steps to pass her. All Chloe saw of the woman passing her were her straight black pants and her flat embroidered slippers. Behind her, at the top of the steps, were two glass doors. The door to the left had "for rent" painted on a sign inside of the glass. It would have been hard to see from the street but sitting here on the steps you couldn't miss it.

Chloe collected herself, rose, and mounted the stairs.

"Please, please, please," she whispered silently to herself.

She knocked three times and waited patiently. If there had been anything worth seeing inside there would probably have been a curtain in the window. There was no curtain and Chloe could see straight down a long empty hall with nothing but a blank wall on the right side and three open doorways on the left. The blank wall was the divider between the two apartments of the narrow building. Chloe waited hopefully in front of the two front doors.

Chloe knocked again. This time a face appeared from the doorway at the far end end of the hall, then a hand appeared next to it and waved. Both disappeared for a moment. Mr. Lu reappeared, hurried down the hall, and opened the door.

"Hello, hello," he said. "I was just fixing a pipe. May I help you?"

"I saw your sign," said Chloe. "My mother and I are looking for a place to live."

"Where is your mother?" he asked.

"She's looking on the next street," smiled Chloe.

Chloe had anticipated the question and lied expertly. She could actually visualize her mother pounding on a door as she spoke.

"I'm meeting her in an hour to compare notes," she added.

Mr. Lu paused.

"OK," he said. "I'll show you around and you tell her how much you love it. Tell her it's the best apartment you ever saw." He chuckled amiably.

"I'm Mr. Lu," he added.

"I'm Chloe," Chloe said as she crossed the threshold.

"There are two bedrooms, a kitchen, and a sitting room," he said as she entered. "Is it just the two of you or are there more? If there are more than two, it can be three bedrooms and a kitchen."

"Just the two of us," Chloe responded.

He stepped into the first room, empty but for a gas heater, raised slightly off the floor and surrounded by pale green tiles mounted on the wall.

Chloe ran to the bay window at the front of the house. She could see down onto the sidewalk and up and down the entire street. She just stood there, looking.

"Did you want to see the rest?" asked Mr. Lu with a smile.

Chloe turned and followed him.

The second room was very small. It had a window on the right and no closet. Through the window came a breeze. Carried lightly on the breeze was the sound of strange, oriental (she assumed) music.

The kitchen was small and awkward, with a door to the fire escape and a window next to the sink. The door to the third room was straight to the back. The apartment curved a bit so that, from the kitchen window, Chloe could see outside, past the wooden fire escape, and in through the opposite window to the small sitting room.

They squeezed around the kitchen table and into the back bedroom. Chloe walked across the room

She stopped before another set of bay windows. She looked down at the garden below. A sea of giant, white calla lilies waved back up at her.

"Those beauties don't grow in the Midwest. They need the warmer winters of San Francisco and similar climates," Mr. Lu told her.

"We'll take it," Chloe said, immediately.

∞

Chloe found Gloria still half asleep. She was reluctant to go out. "Let's go tomorrow," she yawned.

"I already gave him the check mother. What a waste of money if we don't move in. There's a time limit," Chloe lied. A new Chloe was emerging, one that could, in a pinch, speak her mind and fabricate the truth.

The issue of the apartment was already settled, they both knew that. The argument was perfunctory and primarily related to the position of greater authority, which recently had been bantered about between Chloe and Gloria on a regular basis. It took Gloria all the restraint she could muster not to leap up and skip joyously around the room. It just wasn't time yet for her to make the move to agree.

Chloe, too, knew what they were really discussing and the importance of waltzing around the issue until Gloria believed that she held the dominant position. They were engaged in the same game but winning and the path to it were entirely different for each of them. In the end, they both wanted Gloria to feel she was in charge, which, at any given moment, was debatable.

Chloe glanced at her watch. She retained the time element as a secret weapon. She would toss it on the board in about five minutes, lie about it and maneuver her mother to the finish line with time to spare.

Gloria was torn. She wanted to yell at Chloe for forging the check but knew that she couldn't possibly do that. She had taught her the art of forgery. She needed Chloe to take control at times like these. A fair amount of empty arguing went on before Chloe again looked at her watch and in a dramatic tour de force shouted, "we only have five minutes left!"

Off they went.

They dashed down California Street and arrived at the apartment out of breath and just in the nick of time. Well, that's what Gloria was led to believe. Chloe knew that Mr. Lu lived in the apartment next door and he had told her he would be up late. He had not even gone home yet.

Gloria was her best, smiling self and quickly signed the appropriate paperwork. She was glad to find the apartment immaculately clean and partially furnished. There were a single bed, a double bed, two dressers and a modest kitchen table with chairs. Mr. Lu kindly provided bedding when he discovered they had none.

Gloria took the front room, the largest of the three. Chloe took the back bedroom overlooking the garden. The smaller middle room they intended to use as a living room.

It took them about five minutes to unpack their respective paper bags of clothes into their respective dressers. They were tired but hungry and caught the next cable car to an excellent restaurant in Chinatown. They celebrated over mu shoo pork and cashew chicken. Chloe was finding it increasingly unnecessary to prepare conversational note cards, though she still carried two everywhere they went. The two she carried this night were about cycles of the moon and yeti, respectively. She left them unused under her plate with the tip.

They got off the car at Huntington Park and walked the last two blocks down to their new home. They walked on the north side of the street past Grace Cathedral, more apartment buildings and a small Vietnamese restaurant. When they reached a boutique named Twins, they crossed the street to their own apartment.

They were in bed early and dropped off to sleep instantly.

21

UNION SQUARE

"Rise and shine" shouted the cable car a 6 am. It's metallic, clanking voice forced Gloria to drag her bedding into the middle room and sleep another two hours on the floor. She wasn't exactly cranky when she got up, but she wasn't thrilled to find her choice of bedrooms was seriously flawed. She put the coffee on and considered the situation. She loved the big front room. The window provided a view both up the hill and down. She was grateful for the gas heater that kept the room toasty warm even, in what Gloria was discovering, was San Francisco's characteristically chilly, dank weather. But the cable car, "ARRGH"!.

"Earplugs," she said to herself, "That should do the trick. Where on earth will I find earplugs? Chloe will know."

She asked Chloe over breakfast. Mr. Lu had dropped off bagels and cream cheese as well as a couple of packages of coffee and hot chocolate like the kind you find in motels. His wife had insisted.

Chloe gave Gloria a blank, not yet quite awake, look.

"I don't have any idea. Maybe a hardware store."

"Well, we've got to find some. As soon as we're dressed, we're going shopping.

And they did.

According to the map of the cable car lines that Gloria had picked up the night before, they could transfer from the California Street line to the Powell Street line and go directly to Union Square. It mentioned shopping in Union Square.

"Let's give it a try", she said.

And they did.

How adept they had become at hoping on a car even during the briefest of stops. They transferred to the Powell Street car in Chinatown and continued to the end of the line, Union Square.

Shops indeed! What an understatement! This was the age of department stores and Union Square was the place to find them. I Magnin, christened "The Marble Palace" by Christian Dior, opened on Union Square in 1948. A young Mary Ann Magnin ratcheted her small children's store into one of the most elegant, high end clothing and beauty product establishments in America. She affectionately named it after her husband, Isaac. It wasn't long before Mary Ann's store became a chain of luxury stores that spread across the United States.

The Emporium was a seven-story behemoth that stretched for an entire block. Its neoclassical structure housed a mercantile complex so huge it could take your breath away. It contained a vast variety of shops which provided everything from bridal dresses to pets. Carpets, sportswear, books, televisions, women's clothing, children's clothing and everything in between could be found at The Emporium. Not as luxury oriented, sophisticated, or generally as expensive as either The City of Paris or I Magnin, it eventually became Gloria's go to place for towels, linens, and everyday underwear. The furniture she later chose for the living room was delivered from The Emporium.

In 1850 Felix and his brother Emile Verdier sailed their heavily laden ship, The City of Paris, into San Francisco Bay. The Gold Rush was in full swing. The brothers were wildly successful. Their cargo of French lace, clothing, dry goods, and fine wines and champagnes never reached their store on the waterfront. They sold out directly from the ship. The Verdiers turned back to France to fill the ship a second time and in 1851 were again met with great success. They eventually opened The City of Paris Dry Goods Company, a high-end department store, at the corner of Geary and Stockton on Union Square. It was still thriving.

Gloria could hardly wait to get started.

We have come to the right place!" she exclaimed..

Chloe grasped her mother's arm and pulled her toward the center of the square itself.

"Give me just a few minutes," she said as she walked over to the grass, not waiting for an answer.

In the center of the grassy 2 ½ acre public square stood a monument with a stature on top. Chloe read the black and gold plaque. The square was named for the prounion rallies that were held there during the Civil War, the plaque explained. The monument was a tribute to Admiral George Dewey for his success in Manila in the Spanish American War and in memory of President William McKinley, who at the time of the monument's construction, had been recently assassinated. Chloe loved reading this sort of thing.

The final paragraph revealed that the 83-foot pillar was topped with a nine-foot statue of Nike, Goddess of Victory.

"Excellent," thought Chloe. "What's not to like about Union Square?"

Then the shopping began.

Upon entering The City of Paris, they found themselves in the six-story high, open rotunda which was capped by a magnificent stained-glass dome. Each of the six floors was accessed by an elevator. On each floor a woman, dressed in uniform, with the aid of her baton, helped customers on and off the elevator in an orderly fashion. A balcony on each floor allowed customers the excitement of looking up and down the rotunda without falling to their deaths.

On the third floor was a dress shop, a shoe store, and a blouse boutique. Gloria was in heaven.

Gloria held up a silky red dress covered with poppies, large and small.

"Oh, no." exclaimed Chloe, "not that!"

"But I love it," said Gloria. "Life is too short not to wear what you love."

She tried it on for Chloe to see.

"My god. The stress and panic diet paid off," thought Chloe. She looks great!"

"You make that dress look good," she told her mother, enthusiastically.

"Your turn," said Gloria.

Chloe had outgrown the children's section so Gloria took her up to the junior girls section on the second floor. Her mother dragged her to the dress section. Chloe resisted vehemently. She refused to try on a single one. The best Gloria could talk her into were a sky-blue skirt and a navy cardigan to wear with it. When Chloe wasn't looking, she slipped an adorable dress across the check-out counter and then into her own bag. She knew it was futile but she couldn't resist.

"This is not my style," Chloe announced, as she looked through the fashionable pants and sophisticated blouses that The City of Paris had to offer.

"Oh, Chloe, really?" sighed Gloria with disappointment.

She cheered up immediately.

"There are more stores out there," she said with enthusiasm. "Lunch first."

"No, " said Chloe firmly, "first we go all the way up to the sixth floor and look over the balcony."

"Excellent idea," agreed Gloria. Afterward, they had lunch on the first floor at Normandy Lane. While they ate, I Magnin sang her siren song. They answered loud and clear.

Chloe turned out to be much more of an I Magnin kind of girl than a City of Paris one. Although her interest in skirts and dresses was still close to none at all, the slacks were perfect. She could, and did, buy several pairs in both wool and in cotton. They were displayed on a rack in ascending colors of the rainbow. How could she resist?!

The rainbow Chloe chose was a muted rainbow, probably hidden by fog, but a rainbow none the less. Gloria, in a last minute show of practicality, threw in socks, underwear and a pair of shoes. The size she had to guess at because Chloe would not try any on.

Gloria's shopping was limited by two important factors: first, her present unemployment made her ferociously protective of her nest egg; second, she was traveling via cable car. It seemed unwise to risk death by cable car for the sake of carrying one more pair of shoes, no matter how divine they might be.

They were about to board the next car when Chloe remembered the ear plugs.

They were standing outside the Sleep Boutique.

"Can't hurt to try," said Gloria.

Inside there were silk pajamas, lace underwear and satin robes beyond belief. Gloria tried not to become distracted, but it was oh, so hard.

She explained her desperate need for sleep to the sympathetic salesgirl.

"I have just the thing," she said. "Follow me."

In a glass case next to the bejeweled sleep masks were a variety of downy, satin lined, feathery earmuffs. Gloria could hardly choose among them. She tried on the fuzzy, lavender pair with the soft pink lining.

She bought two pairs.

And so ended what came to be known forever in Gloria's mind as The Day of Shopping and Joy.

*

22

SLEEPLESS

"Blasted cable car", her brain mumbled, followed by her audible screams of, " Oh God, make it stop!" the adorable ear muffs were not doing their job. The incessant dinging and rattling began every morning at 6:00 am outside her cute bay window ever since they had moved in on Friday. Now it was only Sunday but it seemed days longer. Gloria was ready to throw herself on the tracks from sleep deprivation. She had napped in Chloe's room that afternoon. Her circadian cycle was completely on the blink. Now it was midnight and she was wide awake with nothing to do.

She got out of bed and sat in the window looking out. Everything was shiny-wet again. The entire block had an alien lime-green glow from the reflections of the apartment buildings on the oil and water slick that glazed the black asphalt. There were still some scattered lights on in the windows of the apartment buildings across the street. Further up the hill things were quiet. Downhill she could see the giant sign from the market glaring up at her from its tower in the parking lot on the corner across the street.

She wanted a bottle of Coke. If she couldn't sleep she might as well wake up. This in-between, night-of-the-living dead feeling had to go.

Wondering vaguely if she'd be stabbed to death going out alone at night in this neighborhood, Gloria pulled on her orange spotted middy top and white capris from the laundry basket. and slipped out the front door, checking the lock as she left. At the bottom of the steps she paused and shivered. This was night as she remembered it, familiar in essence if not in particulars. No stars marred the sky and the darkness only hinted at night. (Goodbye Nevada, and good riddance.) Still, it lacked that familiar pastel, pink glow she associated with Chicago. And she could smell the ocean in the fog. This was a new sensation. She liked it.

"A good thing I didn't drive," she said out loud as she approached the completely packed parking lot. She glanced at her watch...12:15. Odd. A tide of people flowed in and out apparently unaware of their inappropriate timing. Did they too have transit associated sleep deprivation? All of them?

She crossed into the market only to discover what the attraction was. This wasn't just a grocery store it was an all-night party, and not just any party. Full costume was required.

"And I thought I was just going out for a Coke," she thought, no longer needing the caffeine to wake up but somehow craving it more than ever.

She began searching for the beverage aisle, feigning nonchalance, but found it a little disarming to find herself in the narrow grocery store isle among the potato chips, the chicken noodle soup and the man in the bouffant hair-do. Fortunately, her eyes landed on his truly stunning handbag and she suddenly felt right at home.

She blurted out that the bag was divine. She commented on how well it went with his gloves. She couldn't resist adding that if he occasionally twisted his skirt up a little higher his calves and thighs would be more visible. This was, after all, her own personal specialty. She could see from this man's facial structure that nice thighs were part of the package.

They met again at the checkout. The exceptionally colorful and memorable line of men? women? (Gloria wasn't sure) was long enough for them to have time to exchange first names. He voiced his admiration for her capris, which had apparently only become repugnant to her. They continued to talked fashion for a moment before Marten pointed out his friend, Joel, across the way. He was having trouble finding Joel a purse to match his pumps. It was to be a thank you gift for Joel for redecorating their apartment.

Before she could stop herself Gloria blurted out that she had just the thing only half-a-block away. She bought it only yesterday. It was petite and would go well with his relatively small bones and slender waist (which she found herself annoyingly jealous of). Before she knew what she was doing she offered to trade her purse for his boa.

That was when it dawned on her, she really did have skills and there was a market for them. Hmmm.

It was drizzling again as the three of them walked to her front steps. Marten and Joel were laughing lightly and singing softly, "Singin' in the rain, just singin' in the rain…." Gloria wondered momentarily if she had lost her mind. Her sense of insanity, however, was allayed by the talk of apparel and accessories, and the reassuring way Marten did the smiling hair toss maneuver it had taken her so long to master as a teen.

The boys waited under one of the ornamental cherry trees that lined the street in front of Gloria's apartment. Devoid of leaves it offered no protection from the light rain but the couple felt comfortably intimate leaning against its trunk and sharing a cigarette while they waited for Gloria to return.

Gloria practically skipped up the steps with plans for her future bubbling in her head. Skills, she had skills. Her spirit rejoiced.

She reached the two doors that stood side by side, as they frequently do in old Victorian buildings in this city, and opened the one on the left. (The building could not have been more cleanly cut in half). Gloria tip-toed down the hall, slipped on the bare wood floor, and careened around the corner into the second room, where the pile of boxes from yesterday's shopping spree lay strewn everywhere. Most of her purchases were still in the boxes or draped over the furniture to be admired before proper hanging.

Quickly scanning the melee, she spied the accessory section on the coffee table near the window. There in the company of the alligator belt and the ceramic palm tree necklace was the black beaded purse with the rose in full bloom stitched on both sides. It was a perfect match for Joel's adorable pumps with the rose buds on the toes.

Gloria picked up the purse for Martin and a jacket for herself. She took a moment to breathe and departed as she had come, the old floor creaking with every step. She looked through the glass of her front door at the two men waiting for her. "Too bad," she thought, "that Martin is really cute, and funny, too. Just my luck."

She tucked the beaded purse under her jacket to protect it from what was becoming a down pour and called Martin and Joel up the steps to the protection of the entryway. They made their trade, admired their respective prizes and talked a bit more before Gloria retired. Joel and Martin headed home serpentining in and out of doorways dodging raindrops all the way home.

It was 2 am before Gloria's head hit the pillow that she had tossed on the floor of the smaller middle room along with the blankets from her bed. She intended to sleep in. When she did rise, the first thing she intended to do was make this her bedroom. She drifted off to sleep, her new black feather boa around her neck, surrounded by all those clothes that made her look great. While she slept the seed of a glorious plan began to germinate in the misty, fields of her dreams. Life was good.

23

CAHOOTS

Chloe had been watching the school buses come and go since Monday. They stopped at Huntington Park twice a day. She could see them through the front windows. On Thursday her mother noticed them too.

"My God, Chloe, you should be in school. Why didn't you say something?"

"I don't want to go," she replied.

"You can't be shy about this, Chloe. You have to go to school. I'll make phone calls tomorrow and you can catch that bus on Monday."

"In a pig's eye," thought Chloe. She had already decided not to take THAT bus. Not Monday. Not ever.

Gloria talked to the school on Friday and on Saturday she splurged and called a taxi for a reconnaissance run.

"Well, it's not *too* big and it's not *too* far away," Gloria lied when they finally got there.

The office was open until noon on Saturdays, so they picked up the enrollment paperwork and filled it out over lunch.

"Take them with you on Monday," said Gloria.

Chloe said nothing.

Tuesday morning was shrouded in mist, as usual. Chloe wore her navy blue slacks, white blouse and tennis shoes. She buttoned up her navy blue cardigan. As she left the apartment, she looked up at her mother in the bay window. Gloria waved. Chloe reluctantly waved back. Off to school she went.

When she reached the park, Chloe quickly tied her hair back at the nape of her neck and tucked it into her blouse. She tied her new blue cardigan around her neck and stepped to the end of the bus line. When the driver nodded to Chloe to board she shook her head, 'no'. The bus with "San Francisco School District" written on the side rolled away. The bus with "St. Cecelia's Catholic School" written on the side was revealed behind it. Chloe slid between two taller boys in their blue pants, white shirts and blue sweaters and boarded the bus.

The bus driver was preoccupied with adjusting his mirrors and took no notice of her. She moved quickly to the very back of the bus and sat quietly in the corner, looking out the window. She was too intimidated to actually look at the other children. She felt, somehow, that if she didn't look at them, they could not see her.

Around the park they drove and down California Street to Van Ness Avenue. She didn't know where she was going but she was sure she would be back by 4:00. The bus was always back by 4:00. She just had to be sure she was on it. How bad could it be? She was going to a school not the middle of a blazing hot desert. She had already done that. What could go wrong?

"Anna Claire! Back of the bus!" boomed the bus driver shortly after they left the park.

Anna Claire didn't have to ask why. She had thrown confetti all over the bus yesterday as a celebration for a friend's birthday. They were on their way home and the bus driver had to work late to clean it up. He was definitely unhappy with her.

She dropped into the rear seat in the corner opposite Chloe. After a few minutes she slid up right next to Chloe.

"You're not a boy and you don't belong on this bus," she whispered in Chloe ear with admiration. "You're a stowaway!"

The girl found this very exciting. Her eyes sparkled at the thought of adventure.

Chloe froze. The girl slid closer and slipped her arm into Chloe's. "Don't worry. I won't tell," she said. "We can be in cahoots."

Chloe sensed she had rapidly gone from stowaway to prisoner.

"Where are we going?" she asked the girl.

"You don't know? You are a brave one," the girl proclaimed with admiration.

"I'm Anna Claire, Annie to my friends, and we are going to St. Cecilia's. But I guess you knew that part. It says that on that side of the bus. We're on our way to Mt. Tam on the other side of Mill Valley. Doesn't take long, maybe another fifteen minutes.

"Anyway," she continued, "my dad is James Windemere III, ambassador to wherever they want him to go at any particular time. My mom's name is Felicity. Now there's a misnomer. Do you know what a misnomer is?"

Chloe nodded, thinking, "Sounds like this girl hasn't talked to anyone in a week!"

"Not that I don't like her, I do. But she should have been named 'Tempest', or maybe 'Heartbreaker'. She's beautiful and men are always falling at her feet but she sticks like glue to my dad. They're a little nauseating."

"Mine were nauseating too, but in an entirely different way. That's why we left him in Illinois and came here," Chloe said unexpectedly.

"Oh my God." Chloe thought to herself. "What am I doing?! I Don't even know this person and I went and said THAT!"

Chloe fell silent for a long time and gazed out the window. Annie continued to talk intermittently, mostly as a tour guide. The bus stopped occasionally to pick up passengers.

"Look at the sailboats to your right. Aren't they beautiful?"

It was a rhetorical question. Annie left no space for a reply even if Chloe had been inclined to speak.

"Here comes the bridge," announced Annie. "The famous Golden Gate Bridge. You're going to love this."

And Chloe did. Annie paused for a few minutes as they both looked out at San Francisco Bay. The steel cables of the bridge reached to the sky and the water below stretched out on and on. The bus shook every time they crossed an expansion joint.

"St. Cecelia's Catholic School, grades seven through twelve. Won't be long now." announced Annie. 'Costs more to send her to St. Cecelia's than to college!' That's my father speaking"

"Well I won't actually be attending, technically speaking," Chloe was thinking.

"But you won't actually be attending, technically speaking," said Annie.

"Psychic! She's psychic!! Oh no," thought Chloe.

"Do you like boats? You'd be seeing more of them if it weren't for the fog. Well do you?" asked Annie.

"I don't know. I've never been on one," replied Chloe.

"Sharks out there," said Annie. "Don't let anyone talk you into swimming in the bay."

"Can't swim," thought Chloe to herself. She didn't want to admit that out loud.

The fog was still rolling across the hillsides of Marin County as they left the bridge and headed for a tunnel in the hillside.

"I love the tunnel." said Annie.

Then she was silent and they were engulfed in darkness. Chloe found herself grabbing Annie's hand and holding it tightly. It was a long tunnel.

Daylight returned. Chloe dropped Annie's hand in embarrassment.

"That's OK," said Annie.

Then both girls were quiet for some time.

"Everything is so green," thought Chloe.

She looked up the hillside to the left. This was a jungle to her. None of the trees and shrubs were familiar. Giant, emerald leaves and vines tumble down the hills. Huckleberry bushes were beginning to turn autumn purple. The smell of eucalyptus was everywhere. It smelled real and fresh, unlike the lip balm and lotions that she had smelled. In Illinois she could have recognized oaks, elms and pine trees, but this all seemed so...tropical.

They passed signs saying Tiburon and Sausalito. They passed one that said Mill Valley. They were in town and out of town in a flash and up, up the side of Mount Tamalpais they went...

Chloe looked out at the side of Mount Tam. "This is not a mountain." She thought. "I have recently seen mountains, and this is not them." However, she always appreciated any increase in altitude so she accepted it for what it was.

"We're here," said Annie, as she hoisted her book bag to her shoulders.

"Go hide in the bamboo stand over there until the bell rings. Then you're free to roam. I'll meet you back at the bamboo at lunch. I'll bring dessert."

And Annie was gone.

"How am I supposed to know what a stand of bamboo looks like?" thought Chloe. She tried to picture pandas in China and got a general idea. She entered the bamboo and found that bamboo is not soft and cuddly. Fortunately, the stand was not thick and when she came out the other side there was a field of tall grass and yellow wildflowers. She turned back and peeked out at the school.

The main hall of the school was introduced with a series of stone steps and Greek pillars. On each step was a statue of a saint. "It's Mount Olympus," Chloe marveled. "I like it." These were, of course, not statues of Greek gods. This was, after all, a Catholic school. But the statues of St. Cecilia and the other saints were reminiscent of the Greek gods and goddesses Chloe so loved. She took this as a sign.

"I belong here, "she whispered.

Chloe spent her first day at St. Cecilia's trying to remain invisible. She explored the campus, as best she could, by dashing from tree to tree, bush to bush, building to building. She peeked in windows and listened at doors. She listened to the teachers questioning the students.

"I know that one! I know that one!" she whispered, longing to shout out the answer.

Just after lunch, Annie and Chloe sat in the field beyond the bamboo and ate their brownies. Annie pointed out that getting Chloe back on the bus to go home might be a lot more difficult than getting on at Huntington Park and getting to school had been. There would be a lot of kids around looking for their buses and a number of teachers supervising. The kids would be easy enough to work around but the teachers must be avoided at all costs. There were quite a few kids getting on Chloe's bus. The one's from Huntington Park were the first to get on in the morning and the last to get off in the afternoon.

That's a good thing, " said Annie.

"It is?" said Chloe.

"Sure. I'm not a nobody at this school. I have a few friends to help us. Trust me. We are on Bus 12 and we leave second because we have to go so far. Bus nine goes first because they have to go all the way to San Rafael. Anyway, at 3:00 you must, and I mean must, stand over at the far end of the main building, over by the bushes with the red berries. Face away from everybody and be patient. The bus leaves at 3:15. We'll come and get you."

"Trust me," she said, again. "Gotta run."

Annie was having the time of her life. This was better than shoplifting. Annie had orchestrated a flock of girls from Bus 12 to surround Chloe. They joked and waved their sweaters and laughed and hustled Chloe right under the nose of Sister Agnes, who was being distracted by young Phyllis, who faked dropping her books by accident and was sobbing because her papers were blowing away. As Sister Agnes was bent over retrieving essays, Chloe was whisked onto the bus and six students shoved their way on right behind her. At this point half of Bus 12 was in cahoots.

The second day Chloe went to St. Cecilia's she made an important strategical move. On the bus ride to school Annie had enumerated many of her escapades and explained that if you confess to the priest he is bound by his vows not to tell anybody. Also, the rain just would not stop and the bamboo really was pretty poor cover compared to the chapel. Chloe tumbled soaking wet, out of the rain, into the Blessed Children's Chapel and into the heart of Father Ignatius. She asked immediately for confession and she confessed every day after that just to make sure the father would not find a loop-hole.

Annie popped her head into the bamboo. It was Chloe's third day at St. Cecelia's.

"Its time you met Evelyn, she's my best friend and she's just your size. Evelyn stepped through the bamboo and onto the grass. Her hair was long and shiny black, her skin was beautifully white, and her slightly almond eyes were a deep brown. She was holding a blue and white plaid skirt, white blouse, and white knee socks.

"Nice to meet you," she said. "These are for you."

"Now we can all three be in cahoots," said Annie enthusiastically. "I can't stay. I have a meeting with my math teacher. You two get to know each other. Then she was gone.

Chloe and Evelyn looked at each other. Neither knew quite what to say.

"I'm Evelyn," Evelyn finally said.

"I'm Chloe," said Chloe.

The sat down and Evelyn handed the uniform to Chloe.

"Annie and I were talking. I hope you don't mind us talking about you. We thought if you wore a uniform you might eventually be accepted as a student here," said Evelyn.

"But I'm not in anybody's classes and I'm not on anybody's roll call. They'll find me out instantly," countered Chloe.

"No. No they won't," said Evelyn. "You won't actually go into any classes we just want you accepted on campus so you don't have to sneak around. If you only show yourself on the edge of things with me or Annie now and then, everyone will just think that you're not in their classes but you must be in someone else's classes."

Chloe was skeptical but at least the uniform would help her get on the bus every day. She agreed to give it a try.

"Nice to meet you," said Evelyn again, and she too was gone.

Afternoon classes began. Chloe picked up a book from her pile and went to confess.

The father was expecting her. He was looking forward to seeing her. His duties at the school were not that complex. Matins in the mornings, vespers in the evening and mass on Sundays. Of course, he must be available for confessions upon demand. There was not a big demand.

He kept a beautiful flower and herb garden. He prided himself in doing rather nice water colors. Nevertheless he still seemed to have a lot of free time on his hands. Now he had Chloe.

Chloe didn't actually trust the father yet, but she was beginning to like him. In his vestment he sort of resembled a large, black teddy bear. His vestment was tailor made because he could never have bought his size off the rack and there was no big and tall clothing store for the priesthood. His double chin rolled out over his collar and, flanked by his rosy round checks, his warm smile was displayed perfectly.

The smile was genuine. The father was a kind man. Unable to notify anyone of Chloe's presence, he felt a huge responsibility for her well-being. He also found her very likable. The father was a great listener and, it turned out, a wonderful tutor.

Chloe needed books. Evelyn checked out science and English textbooks from the school library saying that she had left hers at a friend's house. Annie checked out math and history texts saying that she had left hers on the bus. Occasionally, Annie or Evy handed in an essay written by Chloe as if it were their own, just to keep Chloe aware of her academic standing. She was always at the top of the class. Every afternoon, right after confession, Chloe and Father Ignatius studied.

She really did not need to confess every day. The father, at this point, had no desire to expose her. He did, however, keep close tabs on her. He made sure Annie and Evelyn watched out for her, got her safely on the bus in both directions, and kept in touch with her throughout the day. The afternoon that she failed to show up for her studies the father was almost in a panic. He lied to get Annie out of class saying she needed to work on her catechism. When she reached the chapel he sent her immediately in search of Chloe. She found

Chloe asleep in the bamboo and sent her straight back to the father. After that she was allowed to nap in the presbytery.

Of the students enrolled at St. Cecelia's, 130 were day students who were driven or bused to school daily. The remaining 70 were boarding students who stayed in the dormitories on campus. Annie had spent time doing each. She was a day student when she was in fifth grade but the following summer her parents threw up their hands and decided to let the sisters take responsibility for keeping her out of reform school.

"I'm not bad," explained Annie, "I was just so excruciatingly bored. You don't know what it's like just bouncing around the penthouse of the Fairmont with a nanny. A nanny! All day long! You'd think I was an infant. So I sneaked down the service elevator a few times and did a little shoplifting. Cheap earrings at I Magnin or candy in Chinatown. You would think I had been out stealing gold bricks. Anyway, I just did it for the fun of it. The girls they used to invite over to keep me company were sooo dull. Not a brain among the lot of them. You're different. I can tell. When you think I'm not looking I can see a sparkle in your eye. The wheels are turning. We can have adventures."

"You have no idea how different I am," thought Chloe. "I've had about all the adventure I can handle.

"Evy, you're my best friend but you know you don't like adventure. You like books and messing around in tide pools and collecting shells. Sometimes that turns into an adventure," Annie admitted. "Remember the earthquake when we were at the beach with your parents? It wasn't a big one but it was definitely exciting. Your father kept yelling, 'Get off the beach! Get to higher ground', but the tidal wave never came."

A few days later the three girls were lying under the mimosa tree, all three in their blue plaid skirts, white blouses, and white knee socks. Evelyn was also wearing a blue cardigan. The plan to dress for success had worked like a charm. After about a week of dressing in uniform and sticking mostly to the periphery of activity even a few of the teachers had learned Chloe's name and said "hi" to her when she was passing to the chapel. Each one did assumed that although she wasn't their student, she must be in some other teacher's class.

Chloe felt Annie had misread her. She had had enough adventures for a lifetime. However, she didn't mind "being in cahoots." In her experience her present situation, though definitely an adventure in the eyes of her friends, was no adventure at all. It was just the new norm.

One afternoon, the two girls escaped a study hall to lie in the grass with Chloe. It was her turn to tell an entertaining story. She revealed the adventure of the exploding car at the gift shop and the secret of her role in it. Her friends were awed. Chloe glowed. Maybe she did like adventure, a little bit, after it was over.

That same day the subject of families came up. Chloe was really just listening but the other two were joking around.

"My dad's name is Alexander Fitzhough IV and my mom's name is Charity. It's an old Chinese name." Evelyn teased.

"Oh, it is not," laughed Annie. "It's just Alexander Fitz and your mom's name is Mihana. And she's not Chinese, Chloe, she's Japanese. All Asians are not the same. But how would you know? You're from Illinois."

Chloe was stunned. Alexander Fitz. Mihana. She couldn't say a word. She could hardly think. Annie and Evy then moved the conversation on to something completely different. Chloe was left behind entirely.

"Alexander Fitz," was all she could think. "Mrs. Fitz."

Finally she asked, "Does your grandmother live with you?"

"What?" said Evelyn. "Sure she does. She's wonderful."

The bell rang for classes.

Chloe added quickly, "Tell her about me. Tell her Chloe says 'hello'."

The girls were already walking away.

"Don't forget," called out Chloe. "Chloe says 'hello'."

The next day Evelyn arrived with a letter for Chloe. Chloe didn't open it until later, when she was alone in the chapel.

It read:

Dear, Dear Chloe,

How did you get here? I have missed you so much. I am so glad you are safe. You must come and see me soon.

Much, Much Love,

Mrs. Fitz

24

THE PLAN

And Gloria? What was she doing while her daughter was AWOL?

Shopping, of course, she was on a mission. This time when she got off at Union Square she made a beeline for the third floor of City of Paris. She purchased one, single, fine outfit that closely resemble the one that the salesgirl in the women's department was wearing. It was more stylish and looked far better on Gloria, of course, than it would ever look on any of the salesgirls; she was Gloria, after all. She had panache.

Gloria folded her old, new clothes and slipped them into her bag. She stepped into the ladies' room and freshened her hair and makeup. She wore her new, new clothes up to the sixth floor and walked directly into the employment office. She was hired on the spot. That afternoon she stood in the jewelry department among diamond earrings and paste; opal rings and plastic; gold, silver, and nickel. Whatever she chose to wear sold immediately, especially to boyfriends that hoped their girlfriends would look like Gloria. Her commissions were already piling up. Of course, the benefit of buying City of Paris goods from any department at twenty percent off was also an attractive job benefit.

The following day Gloria had lunch on the first floor at Normandy Lane.

"Room for one more?" said a voice.

"Joel, what are you doing here?" Asked Gloria in surprise.

"I work in the men's department. I eat here a lot. What are you doing here? Shopping I presume."

"I, too, have a job," she boasted. "I started in the jewelry department yesterday."

Then they talked best clothes, best buys, commissions and the lovely twenty percent discount.

That was the beginning of shopping madness. Joel was an impeccable model of men's clothing by day and a stylish cross-dresser by night. The two of them spent many a happy lunch hour in and out of union square boutiques spending a large chunk of what they were making. She looked stunning on a regular basis, as did he.

Nor did they neglect I Magnin or the Emporium. They spent so much time in the City of Paris women's department that they were quickly on a first name basis with the salesgirl. Her name was Susan, but she didn't mind being called Susie. Susie was amazing. She could take one look at a customer and go directly to the perfect shade of cloth, the exact size, and the best style. When a new shipment came in, she would slip aside whatever she thought either Gloria or Joel would like because she knew they would be back in a day or two. She became their personal shopper.

"We've got to stop this," said Joel, ten days later. "You are such a bad influence. Marten is going to kill me when he realizes how much money I've spent. On the other hand," he whispered, "he seems to really like the way I look."

"Nobody cares how I look," said Gloria in a brief moment of self-pity.

"I do," said Joel. "I only hang out with the most beautiful people," and he gave her a hug.

"Well, I'd better watch my step then," she laughed. "Remember those shoes at I Magnin? Let's each go buy a pair."

After that Joel began driving Gloria to and from work, if he didn't have to drive the other direction to get Marten to work first.

THE PLAN

"Shopping isn't as exciting as it used to be," confessed Gloria on the way home one day. It was rush hour and even Joel, the most even-tempered man on the planet, was getting frustrated. "Broaden your horizons, woman." He swerved out of the way of an oncoming car. "Go to an art gallery, go to a nightclub, see a movie. You've never even seen Golden Gate Park! This is the big city. If you can't find amusement here, you won't find it anywhere." Then traffic came to a stand still. "I love you, Gloria, but I am not driving tomorrow so you'd better find alternate transportation. I'm taking the cable."

"I don't blame you," said Gloria. "I've never seen it so bad."

"Get Susie to go some where with you," he continued. "She has a couple of little kids at home. I'm sure she'd like a night off. You should ask her."

Traffic started up again and she was home in minutes. Thanks for the lift, Joel I'll take your advice."

"See you tomorrow," he said, and he threw her a kiss.

∞

Susie was apologetic when she declined the invitation. "I do have two kids," she explained. "They're still both really little so my husband and I have to work opposite shifts so someone is always home with them. If we ever do have the same time off we like to spend it together. Thanks though."

It was Friday night. When Chloe came out of her room for dinner Gloria said, "Let's go to a movie."

Chloe couldn't believe her ears. She remained cautiously cool to the idea. "What's playing?"

"Who knows," said Gloria. "Let's walk down to that cinema on Bush Street and find out."

"We should call first," said Chloe.

No, we need to get out. There's bound to be something good on.

It's not far. We can walk down."

It was not far and the night was warmish. Chloe took one look at the movie poster and refused to enter the building. The Birds was playing. Hitchcock's superb thriller was more than Chloe could cope with. Visions of all those birds on the poster attacking while quoting Poe was more than Chloe could take. It was bound to plague her sleep for days, and she knew it. They both agreed that the other movie, the spy movie, To Russia With Love, with Sean Connery, was a far better option. They were not disappointed.

On the way to bed Chloe said, "Good night."

Gloria threw her a kiss.

After Joel and Gloria became shopping buddies, Gloria had a place to go when she couldn't sit home a second longer on a Saturday night. She sent Chloe to bed at nine o'clock and went to Marten and Joel's. Locking the door soundly behind her, she headed uphill to Huntington Park and turned into the apartment building on the left. Their unit was on the second floor overlooking the park. Marten and Joel had friends over most Saturday nights. It was a mixed crowd. She was welcome.

The next day Chloe begged for a phone. She had, of course, not been asleep when her mother left and had lain awake worrying until she finally drifted off alone watching the Twilight Zone on the new television. Gloria was sincerely apologetic. She called the phone guy from the pay phone at the market down the hill and the phone was installed the following Tuesday.

Still, Chloe did not feel entirely secure. She couldn't actually conceive of anything that would constitute as an emergency happening, but just in case she looked up the numbers for the Fire Department and the Police Department in the new phone book. She passed up on the Water Department, the Department of Sanitation, and the

Department of Human Services, she didn't even know what they did. She cut a piece of notebook paper into a perfect square, copied the pertinent numbers neatly on to it and posted it on the refrigerator with a piece of scotch tape. Then she crossed the street to Twins.

Twins had a pink and white stripped awning above the front door with "Twins" written in lime green letters on it. It was owned by two women who were themselves twins and who rarely left each other's side. They were in the process of transitioning into the sale of twin ensembles for adults, but for now they only sold clothing for children ages newborn to twelve. Chloe had visited them before. She had been out walking one afternoon and they had invited her in to see the new dresses. It would have been rude to refuse. She would not actually be allowed to buy anything, they explained, because at Twins, not only could you buy two of anything, you were required to do so. They liked twins. Irish twins counted. Chloe tried not to think of all this as peculiar, but she did, because it just was. They offered their sympathy that Chloe was not a twin, but assured her that they liked her anyway, and she was welcome to come and say "hello" any time. Every now and then they all waved at each other from across the busy street.

Chloe told the Twins that her mother was often gone in the evening and, that although she could call the firemen, she would need someplace to go while they were putting out the flames. They agreed wholeheartedly that she should come to them in any emergency. They cautioned her to take special care with the space heaters and loaned her their extra fire extinguisher. They encouraged her to bring it back as soon as she could buy her own. They had another but they really liked having two.

The following Saturday Gloria went again up to Marten and Joel's. Chloe didn't mind, she felt better with the phone at home. She woke up at eleven. It was raining hard. Her mother was still gone. The rain was loud and she felt terribly alone. Chloe called her mother at Marten's.

An unknown voice answered the phone.

"Gloria.your daughter's on the phone," the voice called out.

Pause.

More unknown voices.

Marten's muffled voice could be heard in the background.

"Chloe?" asked her mother. Is that you?"

"Hi," said Chloe softly. "I miss you," she whispered to her mother.

"Did you need something?" asked Gloria.

"No." Chloe said, again softly.

"Here, talk to Marten for a minute," her mother blurted out, before blank air and far away laughter filled Chloe's ear. Then Martin was there, sounding slightly drunk and a little annoyed at finding Chloe on the line.

"Chloe," he said in the loud voice he had been using to joke with someone else over the sound of the music. "How are you?"

"Fine," said Chloe, who felt even more uncomfortable than Martin did.

There was a pause and Chloe could hear Martin talking to someone across the room.

"Here's Gloria," he said, when he finally got back to her.

Before her mother got on the line Chloe realized she had made a big mistake. She didn't miss Gloria at all. She could do without talking to Gloria for a very long time. She hung up without speaking.

In truth, Gloria's nights at Martin's apartment had not been all fun and games. Gloria's evenings were filled with networking, networking, and more networking. While enjoying a night out with her

THE PLAN

new acquaintances she was developing a plan. On her visits Gloria had carefully been studying the dress, accessories, and behaviors of a subculture. In the process she could not help going a little native. She found that she, Marten and Joel all liked the same music, laughed and cried at the same movies, and found the same men attractive. And, let's face it⸺she wouldn't be there in the first place if she and Marten hadn't shared a fashion sense. These acquaintances could turn into actual friends.

The following Saturday night, Gloria asked Joel and Marten for help. She was looking for consultants. They would be paid in gift certificates and discounts. The response was a round of applause and encouragement. Her innate talents had found a niche. Gloria's dream was on the road to becoming a reality. She would open a women's clothing store for men. Evening gowns in men's sizes. Capris in men's sizes, feminine blouses in men's sizes.

The following Saturday night, Gloria arrived with another excellent and closely related epiphany. JCPenny does it, Sears does it, Montgomery Ward does it , why not us. Catalog sales she announced with enthusiasm. This time her enthusiasm was met with skepticism and blank expressions. She still needed consultants, she said, but she also needed a couple of partners; not equal partners, mind you, but partners nonetheless. She looked directly at Joel and Marten, who slipped quietly away into the kitchen before she could make eye contact.

That week no one was beating down the door to be either a consultant or a partner. She stayed home with Chloe while they both did their homework.

"How's school?" Gloria asked cheerfully.

"Fine," answered Chloe in the most noncommittal way she could.

"What do you like best?"

"I like my English teacher," she replied truthfully, thinking of Father Ignatius. That makes the subject interesting. We read a lot."

"What are you reading?" asked Gloria, trying to keep the conversation going.

Chloe realized this required a more creative answer. "Passages in the Bible...ah...compared to Greek mythology," she replied with her fingers crossed. It was only a small stretch of the truth. She was reading both.

"That sounds rather advanced for a ten-year-old," said Gloria, who had never read either, "but I have faith in you. I'm sure you're up to it."

Chloe's heart sang. Her mother had faith in her. She went back to reading the story of Andromeda and Perseus. It was very exciting. She had just reached the part where Andromeda was chained to the rock, the waves were crashing up against her feet and Poseidon had sent for the sea monster to tear her from the rock and devour her.

Gloria went back to designing a clothing catalog. It was a women's fashion catalog for men and in men's sizes. So far it lacked undergarments. This is where she really needed Joel. She had learned a couple of things about Joel last week. First, after just one drink he could not stop talking; second, he liked to talk about himself.

Joel's mother had always been very understanding regarding his sexual preferences, his father, not so much. For his fifteenth birthday Joel's father bought him a football signed by Bart Starr. His mother bought him a sewing machine. That Christmas his father bought him tickets to a professional hockey game in St. Paul and the two of them attended together. His mother gave him a gift certificate to the fabric store. After high school his father wanted him to go to the University of Minnesota. His mother supported his decision to go to San Francisco School of Design. His father in denial to the end, shook his hand and patted him warmly on the back when he left. His mother bought him a new car and parked it down the street, hidden around the corner, where the taxi dropped him off. She cried when he left.

Marten, on the other hand, seemed to have a head for business and marketing. Currently he sold cars at a place on Van Ness Avenue, just a quick ride away on the Muni bus. When she went window shopping for a new car she had seen him in action. ("Just window shopping. Just window shopping," she reminded herself.) He was very impressive. He was as good at selling cars as Susie was at selling clothing, maybe better. He knew how to pick a selling point and make the customer think that that point, and a few others, were what they had come in for. That these points were their idea. After they agreed the car was perfect, he would talk them into all the extras. They always left happy, no matter how much they had spent. He knew his clientele.

Gloria planned on selecting and designing clothing herself, well some of it. She knew Joel would want a part in that, too. She needed him more than she initially imagined. Her concepts were good but her drawings were not.

"That's a dressy, black pencil skirt with adjustable padding at the hips and derriere," she told him.

"You could have fooled me," he said.

He redrew it and added a long row of small round black buttons down the front.

They could be left open at any point down the front of the skirt. He added fluffy ruffles at the hips.

"This is a simple, casual, navy blue skirt. Very short," she told Joel. "You can see it already has a row of red buttons down the front and comes with a red, leather belt."

This drawing was better, Joel lied. Then she showed him the full length, ecru evening gown with lace bodice and a diamond cutout on the back.

"Revealing yet sophisticated," he said, "but you can't draw worth beans." He quickly sketched a few models into the clothes Gloria had drawn. He put all three drawings in a drawer to look at later.

"OK," he finally said. "I'm in, But only as a consultant. No big responsibilities. You have to consider what I like, too. We can work on the catalog but you have to figure out how we'll pull this all off. Don't get me excited and then let me down. And I'm not quitting my job. If I end up working more than four hours a week I want cash, not gift certificates and discounts."

When they talked to Marten he was still not sold on her grand idea. "Money, Gloria, where is the money coming from? I don't have any. Joel doesn't have any. How will you pay for inventory? How will you pay for a storefront? How will you print your catalog? Pipe dreams. Waste of time."

"By the way," he said brusquely, "my consultant fees start now. So listen carefully. You have to have a better understanding of your target customers. Your store should also have casual men's clothing as well as women's clothing for men. All gays are not cross-dressers. Wouldn't hurt to throw in costumes for everybody. Everybody loves costumes. Work in some accessories; jewelry, scarves and bags."

"I'm sorry I offended you, Marten. For me, this is all about the clothes. I see a lot of guys out there who like women's clothing. I like women's clothing. I've studied women's clothing all my life. I think we can start a business and have some fun doing it. Lighten up, Let me get you another drink, maybe not so strong." They all laughed. They turned the music up, she admired the art on the walls and this time she was home by midnight.

THE PLAN

Gloria took everyone's advice to heart. When her clothing store opened on Polk Street in time for Halloween, it had a picture window on either side of the front door. The window to the left read "Men's Clothing". The window to the right read "Women's Clothing for Men". Above the door was a sign which read, loud and clear, GLORY, in big letters, under which was printed, though smaller, 'Costumes for All'.

The early opening on October 21, was for costumes only and the first catalog reflected that. The sales were phenomenal. Flamboyant was the name of the game. Halloween, of course, was the big money maker in the Queer community. Halloween was to Glory as Valentines' Day is to FTD. The Delft blue Dutch girl costumes with fat braids falling from under enormous, white hats came with huge, faux, wooden clogs and were a winner. Giant, yellow, bananas with openings for the face, arms and legs were displayed in the window. Elaborate masks of tropical feathers with matching cod pieces and arm bands glimmered in the light. All of these were available at Glory.

Marten reminded them not to forget leather and rubber.

"What?" asked Gloria.

"Oh, Gloria, you are so naive," laughed Marten.

Joel chimed in, "We have to do a Carmen Miranda. I love Carmen Miranda. Her fruit headdress, the little ruffled crop top, the flamenco style skirt. Everybody loves Carmen Miranda."

Most popular of all was the plain, gray, calf length coat with a purple velveteen collar, which flashed opened to reveal, well, anything you wanted it to. It was lined with a shiny gold lamé fabric and the velveteen collar that Gloria herself had once worn was often replaced with colored, downy feathers. Underneath there was room for special orders, customer's choice, It was Gloria's *pièce de résistance*.

And what was the signature, Glory song? Harry Bellafonte sang "Six foot, Seven foot, Eight foot bunch" nine or ten times a day.

The Halloween opening was just a *pre*-grand opening, Only costumes were available for the Halloween rush. As orders poured in, Joel and Marten reconsidered their roles as consultants and became partners. Gloria kept fifty-two percent and Joel and Marten agreed to accept twenty-four percent each.

∞

Gloria had no idea what she was in for. Marten and Joel, on the other hand, had a pretty good idea. Ever since the late 1800's Halloween in San Francisco had been an adult holiday. Elaborate masked balls and extravagant block parties had been held throughout the city. In the 1960's the gay community joined in and held their outlandish version of the same down at North Beach.

San Francisco drew the Queer population from all over the nation. There was an openness in the gay communities around North Beach, Polk Street and the Castro district that made LGBTs feel hopeful. Still, San Francisco was a city whose largely homophobic Irish Catholic police force enthusiastically upheld laws that prohibited Gays from peaceable assembly. Sodomy laws were still on the books and it was illegal for men to dress in women's clothing in public. That is not to say that any of these activities seized to exist, but the police force might enforce these laws at will, whenever they felt like it The result was openness with an air of paranoia. On Halloween, however, North Beach was cordoned off for the biggest, most outlandish, Queer block party in existence. For some unexplained reason at the beginning of the festivities the police chief himself announced "this is your night……you run it." Everyone previously in the closet, out of the closet or standing in the doorway seemed to cast aside common morality and modesty of any kind in order to revel in their sexuality and freedom of choice.

Glory provided a large portion of the costumes paraded on that night. Since time was of the essence, Marten had the sense to hire a small bevy of temporary seamstresses to help out. They had to be willing to work ridiculous hours to fill the barrage of orders that were coming in daily. The costume catalog had been very effective. Sewing machines hummed day and night.

Marten asked repeatedly, "Where is the money coming from?"

Gloria answered by breaking her own cardinal rule, the one regarding the nest egg. She had financed Halloween out of her own pocket and requested full payment up front for special orders. She did it not just to bring in the proceeds from a single event, but to make possible the appointment with the bank two days after Halloween. Marten went along to sign with her since an unaccompanied woman would never be given a loan. It wasn't even legal. The loan officer was unable to hide his personal disgust with the whole business concept but had to admit that it was destined for success. The loan was approved, Gloria signed the paperwork and Glory, LLC was born.

25

BUSINESS

Marten had had the sense and forethought to begin preparing for the Christmas rush before Glory was even open for Halloween. He intended to have everything prepared on paper so that he could burst into action the second Gloria gave him the go ahead. One of the first things he had learned in life was that much of financial success was based on the ability to delegate. He had a notebook of lists of work to assign to Joel, Gloria, and a variety of employees he intended to hire. Marten had always been the *delegatee*, and poorly paid for it. Now he had the opportunity to be the *delegator* and the very thought of it spurred him on to action.

He set up a private office for himself, partitioned off from the general office area above the store. His desk had stacks of notebooks and binders. Some, dedicated to the store, were labeled "clothing", "costumes", "fabrics", "employees", etc. Some were dedicated to school and were labeled according to business, accounting, and marketing classes.

"Marten's father had turned out to be a unexpected wellspring of funds when his son called him to ask for help to return to school. It was a phone call Marten had been loathe to make but it turned out to be a great eyeopener. Marten had misjudged his father entirely. He discovered that his father did not dislike him and judge him harshly for his sexual preferences. He disliked him and judged him harshly for his inability to make a buck, which his father considered a travesty and a stain on the family name. The existence of the shelves of school books and binders could only be attributed to

Marten's father, who's hope it was that, at last, his son might become a wealthy captain of industry, like himself, and one day follow in his own footsteps to become a vice president of U.S. Steel. To this end he not only paid for school, but also sent a monthly stipend enabling Marten to quit his job at the car lot and focus on his education. Glory actually became an ongoing part of that education and constituted the bulk of his senior thesis.

Every time he was assigned a project in which he was to invent a business and manipulated it in some way, he used Glory. In this way he received expert guidance on whatever he planned to do in real life. It was a proverbial "'two birds with one stone" situation. All the things he planned to do to prepare for the Christmas rush was first unknowingly approved of or disapproved of by his professors. He received college credit for presenting a payment plan for a modest number of employees that included health insurance. He compiled a list of clothing sources by delegating the task to Joel. Joel complied by copying information from packing lists from the men's clothing shipments that arrived at City of Paris. Joel hired Susie to do the same from the women's clothing shipments. (Marten was paving the way to stealing her away from City of Paris to work for Glory.)

Every time Joel had an hour free from supervising the seamstresses and designing costumes for Halloween, Marten pushed him to design pieces for the Christmas opening. This is where the twenty percent discount came in. Joel and Gloria consolidated their discounts in order to buy exceptional pieces from City of Paris. Gloria painstakingly took them apart and Joel reconstructed them into newer, better, Frankenstein couture. It was essential that he do so in a way that made them distinctly different from the originals in order to avoid massive law suits.

According to Marten, no women's clothing store is "worth it's salt" without accessories. At Glory this meant primarily hats, wigs, flashy scarves and a smattering of jewelry, earrings in particular. Marten assigned this task to Gloria, who was in a quandary as to how to complete it. Finally, she made a deal with the Twins. The Twins refused to give up their sources but agreed to a favorable arrangement involving exclusivity and a sizable discount. Gloria spent many a night lounging in front of her space heater combing accessory catalogs from Twins.

But where could they purchase exquisite fabrics? Joel was struggling with this. They had no intention of continually building composites from expensive City of Paris clothing. That was only for a few prototypes for the Christmas rush. Joel could design better, but he needed some time. Until then, he could take a particularly beautiful bodice with a deeply folded neckline from an evening gown and attach it to a beautiful, narrow, popular below-the-knee length skirt, add fluffy ruffles around the derriere, pad the hips, change the sleeves a bit and voila, a Chez Glory masterpiece. Now he could reproduce it, if he had the fabric.

But, lo and behold, it was almost the sixties, The Advent of Synthetic Fabrics. "Expensive exotic silks and satins are not required," said the small, red demon on his shoulder.

"But I like them," cried out Joel..

"Well, you can have them but not today" said the little demon.

"Polyester is not as comfortable as cotton and silk," argued Joel.

"That is true," said the little, horned man with the tail, also known as the sales rep who was giving Joel a pitch on the phone, "but in this modern age they are more sought after than natural fabrics."

Joel was unconvinced.

"This is the age of technology," whispered the little devil. "The space program; a man on the moon; beat the Russians at everything; it's what Americans want. Synthetic fabrics represent America's superior technology. Synthetics can be permanently dyed in shockingly brilliant colors and designs that don't fade. They are an easy surface for screen printing and bold designs. Ask Andy Warhol. After the black and white of the 50's the public wants technicolor, shocking technicolor."

Joel reluctantly conceded and bought polyester, rayon, nylon and spandex. The later turned out to be a godsend for Glory's particular clientele. He designed very popular, easy to create, inexpensive pieces that were destined to fly out of the shop. The demon was right, but not entirely.

Joel still longed for real silk, Egyptian cotton and beautiful, soft linens. "Who doesn't want to look like the great film stars of the of the 30's: Marlena Dietrich with her smoky eyes, sequined jackets, silky form fitting dresses, and feathers; Jean Harlow in clingy satins and silks, with fluffy furs and feathers around her neck; Claudette Colbert in her low, form fitting, bodice framed by billowy silk sleeves and poofy boas?" he reasoned. "If you can't sell me the fabrics I'm looking for, little devil, I will go elsewhere." And he did.

"Yay Joel!' shouted the 'two income no children' crowd. "Hang the expense. We want what you want." For these Joel ordered the Egyptian cotton shirts, the silk blouses, and the fine linen suits, which drew customers from all over the city.

True, many of Glory's clientele could not afford exotic silks and imported linen suits, and many did prefer the vibrant, bright styles of the day. Joel provided them. Many were more conservative and stuck to linen weave suits with pleated trousers in a rayon, cotton, and Dacron blend. Joel provided them.

Then there were a special few who combined, in their their own dazzling and memorable way, what Glory offered in a variety of different styles. These rose above the common people to become royalty, these were elevated to the status of Queens.

Success is complicated. Joel worried that the store would not be big enough, So, if all went as planned for Christmas, the three agreed that in January they would increase the floor space by also renting the building next door.

Part of the additional space would be used to display easily ordered items like specialty jeans and t-shirts. Who doesn't like to see a nice pair of buns in a tight pair of jeans? It doesn't matter if they are hip huggers, high waisted, flared, or boot cut, it's the behind that counts. The effect of an impressive exit can be life altering. That and comfort, of course. The baggy buns look held only a flash in the pan popularity among hippies, mod Europeans, and Midwestern college students.

Christmas, however, was not yet upon them and Gloria was already becoming exhausted. "I didn't know he could wield a whip so effectively," commented Gloria wryly, regarding Marten.

"Oh, he's not into that," assured Joel.

"Maybe not at home," said Gloria, "but he's doing a bang up job of waving it above our heads at work often enough. Has he forgotten that we still have other jobs?"

When Joel began to sport dark circles under his eyes, Gloria shouted "ENOUGH!...meeting of the executive branch...that's us... tonight! We'll all be working anyway...."

Chloe spent the night at Annie's. Gloria brought the wine. Joel remembered the importance of cheese and crackers. Marten brought the books. They were right there on his desk anyway.

After a glass or two of wine, Gloria announced, "I am going to celebrate the Christmas season by quitting my job at City of Paris. How about you, Joel?"

"It's either that or get fired," he replied. "I looked so terrible yesterday when I got to work that I almost fired myself."

"Marten, figure out how to pay us more, please." pleaded Gloria.

"Let's take a vote," said Marten.

"You must be kidding," she said. Her vote counted fifty-two percent anyway but they voted just to make him happy.

The vote was three in favor, none against. Marten wrote it down.

"Can't you do something about him? She whispered to Joel.

"He's going to make us rich," Joel whispered back.

Then Marten put his request on the table.

"My turn," he said. "I'm good with numbers, but I'm not an accountant. You are crazy to trust me with the accounts. I'm struggling with this and you two don't even notice. Also, you can't quit your jobs for a couple of weeks because I need money to hire an accountant."

"Accountant...I thought we already had one," said Gloria.

"We do. It's me. And I have a splitting headache most of the time." he said.

"No wonder you're so cranky," said Gloria. "Get the aspirin immediately. They're in my purse, right next to you. I think it's OK to take three or four at a time. I do."

"Well...?" said Marten.

"I think we should... take a vote," said Joel.

The vote was three in favor and none opposed. Marten wrote it down.

Marten spread his books across the table.

"Oh, Marten, do we have to?" chimed in Gloria and Joel in unison.

"Yes. This is a meeting of the board. We must act accordingly." insisted Marten.

"I'm already bored," proclaimed Gloria, whose eyelids were beginning to droop.

"Fine," said Marten "Just look at the titles for now, so you get some idea what it is I do. Neither of you really have any idea what I do. Do you even care?"

"Oh, dear." said Gloria, her sympathy possibly exaggerated by the second glass of wine.

"He feels unappreciated," said Joel, a little distraught at the thought.

"We're sorry," said Gloria as she reached over and poured Marten another glass of wine. "We need to eat."

Around nine o'clock the Thai food arrived and they opened the last of bottle of wine. They toasted each other individually. They toasted themselves as a group. They toasted to the glorious future of Glory.

When they had finished, they sat back in a row on the couch with their legs stretched out in front of them and stared into the candlelight.

"Do you ever, in situations like this...I mean ...not really this situation, but in some similar situation...sit back and think, 'I really have no idea what I am doing?'" asked Marten.

"Frequently, but not in this situation, of course," responded Gloria.

"No, not now...but at other times." said Joel.

"You know maybe in another situation that didn't really crush you with responsibility but in which you might feel quite a bit of weight..." continued Marten.

"Quite a bit, yes," yawned Joel.

Maybe the accountant will know what he's doing," offered Gloria.

"I certainly hope so," said Marten.

Joel said nothing. He was asleep with his head on Marten's shoulder.

∞

A week later, when all their hangovers had healed, Marten called another meeting of the board of directors. He was offering dinner, wine and Gerald Hansen, the accountant. This time Marten brought the wine, just two bottles for the four of them, in order to save everyone from themselves. When Joel closed the store, they all retired upstairs for a glass of wine before more business. Marten introduced Gerald, whom he had met through Franklin, who knew him from the work he did for the costume director at the opera house, whose friend Jody had played a member of the crowd scene in *Barber of Seville* and had also used Gerald as her accountant when she had a financial dispute over a piece of land she had bought in Oregon with a friend. He came with sterling recommendations, albeit a bit through the grapevine.

Gerald was already beginning to feel uncomfortable. He was used to office buildings and conference tables and men in stuffy business suits. He himself was wearing one.

When Marten finally opened up the card table and everyone sat down to listen to what Gerald had to say, Gerald was a little more at ease. He took off his glasses for a moment, to clean them, before he took his magician's hat out of his briefcase and pulled a ledger out of it. None of them had ever seen a ledger before, so they were already impressed.

"He has a ledger," whispered Gloria to Joel.

"He must know what he's doing," said Joel.

He held the ledger above his head and shook it firmly until the money poured out onto the card table. The coins sparkled in the beams of light and the bills flapped their little bill wings until they drifted to rest gently before the Board.

"And that's where you stand," Gerald concluded. Then he smiled broadly and added, "So to answer your questions regarding paychecks, this is what I'm suggesting... quit your outside jobs if you're willing to live on this. He handed them each their first checks.

Marten stopped the paychecks in mid air. "First we have to vote, he said. All in favor of paychecks say " aye", Ayes resounded around the room. All opposed? The room was silent.

"You may accept the paychecks, he announced.

Three hands sprang out before Gerald. .

"We are three satisfied customers," announced Marten as he poured the chenin blanc. It was Marten's belief that all board meetings should include toasts.

Gloria stood and held her glass high.

"To Marten...for his business acumen and his skill in hiring an accountant."

And again.

"To Gerald...for saving me from an unpleasant commute and helping to feed my daughter."

Gerald was pleased to be toasted but was, once again, edging himself towards the door.

"To Gloria..." started Marten.

"Wait!" said Joel. "I propose we offer Gerald a six month contract. We need you Gerald!"

Gerald didn't know what to say. Really. He did *not* know what to say. These three were crazy. They had no training, they had no solid idea what they were doing, and they were so...casual. Then again they seemed to have halos made of dollar signs. He had seen their books. This was probably a good idea as long as he kept a safe distance. He took his hand off the doorknob.

"First we have to vote." announced Marten. There followed four ayes and zero nays.

"Sorry, Gerald. You can't vote," said Marten.

Gerald was disappointed, though he wasn't sure why.

"Cheer up, Gerald," said Marten. "You're hired. Write yourself a contract."

"Marten, I'm an accountant, not a lawyer"

"Do we need one of those?" asked Gloria.

"Probably," replied Joel.

"Marten, get us a lawyer,"

Joel nodded.

"Vote first."

The ayes won.

"Hold on. Can we afford a lawyer?"

"I'll find a way," Gerald promised. "But they don't come cheap."

"Oh dear," cried Joel.

"You may each have to sacrifice something from your paychecks."

"Oh dear," cried Gloria.

"I'll let you know tomorrow."

"Oh dear," cried Marten.

"But it shouldn't be too much. You may want to work part time for just a little while.

A sigh was heard throughout the room.

Gerald tried again to edge himself out the door, but found himself face to face with the Thai delivery guy.

"Always Thai food?" asked Marten.

"It's the best!" chimed in Joel and Gloria.

"They're right you know," said Gerald as he let himself back into the room and allowed his glass to be refilled. "Especially if you get it from that place on California and Hyde."

"Is there any place else?" asked Joel.

So Gerald stayed.

26

HELLOOO

It was midnight. Gloria had given up sleeping in the front room long ago. The earmuffs were superfluous, didn't help one bit. She slept in the middle room. Still, she was awake. She went looking for snacks. Cala Foods beckoned to her. She heard a familiar voice.

"Gloria," Marten called from down the aisle. "What are you doing here…again. You should be asleep. The coat over the bathrobe is not a good look for you."

"Just restless," she said. "If I'd known I would meet you two, I would have worn an evening gown."

"You need company," Joel said. "Someone to keep you at home."

"Not me," replied Gloria. "I've had company. I've even had marriage. It wasn't a pretty picture."

"Now you're just being silly," chimed in Joel.

"Come with us to the Gold Gallery Wednesday night. Our friend Harold has an opening. He's an excellent photographer. I met him at the Art Institute." said Marten. "I was a good student but he actually had vision."

"And he's straight," added Joel.

"You're trying to set me up," exclaimed Gloria.

"What's the harm in that?" chimed in Marten. "I'll admit that we are great company but we are not your destiny. Don't look so worried. There will be a lot of people there. You'll have fun. You could use some fun."

Gloria agreed. "But don't make it obvious," she pleaded. "I'm really not ready for the whole couple's song and dance again."

They picked Gloria up Wednesday at six o'clock. Joel drove.

There was not a huge crowd at The Gold but there was a reasonably good turnout. Gloria was glad she had decided to wear the red, silky, poppy dress that Chloe had initially hated, then loved. It's square neck was just revealing enough to attract attention without being tacky. This was not a tacky, beginner's show. She was also glad that she had worn her hair up; her stockings were the right shade; her shoes were perfect; the clip holding her hair was Christian Dior. She more than fit in.

Harold had quite a following and his work was selling well. He had recently finished a nature shoot in the southwest. Before that he had been to the Galapagos. He possessed a wonderful talent for photographing the natural world. Gloria had come expecting to see nice photos of bears or lizards sitting on rocks. She even expected some nice renditions of birds in the style of Audubon, though Audubon was not really a name she knew. She was not prepared for the stunning effects Harold achieved with the reflections of birds on the water and the swirling motion of flocks in flight. Marten was explaining that some the best light for photographing appeared in the early morning or just before sunset. That was how Harold had captured the glistening rainbow effect on the marine iguana's back He also praised Harold as a " magician in the darkroom".

"These are beautiful," said Gloria. Everyone around her agreed.

The three were about to move on to the images of the Southwest when a voice came from behind them.

"Marten, Joel you came."

"Of course we came. Why should that surprise you?" smiled Marten. "Wouldn't miss it for the world. We brought a friend."

Gloria turned for the introduction. Her smile froze. "It was THAT Harold. THAT HAROLD! Harold Friend of the Maniac in the Desert Harold. It can't be." She quickly turned away and slipped behind a post. "It can't be. Impossible. This is who they want to set me up with??"

Marten saw her and grabbed her hand with a tug. "This is Gloria. She loves your work. Gloria this is Harold who is responsible for all this great photography."

After a long pause, Harold began to laugh uncontrollably. The color drained from Gloria's face. She grabbed a glass of champagne off the tray that was being passed and sipped, and then sipped again. When her color came back and her smile relaxed she too began laughing. It was the only thing to do.

"You two know each other?" Joel was perplexed.

"In a nutshell, she stole my car with me in it," offered Harold.

"I didn't steal it," replied Gloria. "We just sort of borrowed it while you slept. You were still in it when you woke up and we were not, thank God."

"'In it' a hundred miles from where we expected to wake up! Don't worry. We got over it pretty fast. Jack had sobered up and saw a good story in it. He's always looking for a good story."

"You had Jack with you?' said Marten aghast. "No wonder she stole the car and ran away. What about Chloe? Where was she?"

"She was the driver," said Harold.

"Of course, she was," said Joel.

"And it's time to look at Arches National Monument," announced Marten.

27
NOT THE DADDY

Joel used his knee to knock on Chloe's front door. His arms were full of the large boxes he was carrying from his car to the apartment. By some strange twist of fate he had been able to park right in front of the house and was trying to bring six boxes of wigs and a mirror up the steps in only two quick trips.

Joel kicked harder and louder. "Help! Chloe!"

When Chloe opened the door, there was Joel, looking very stylish in his orange wool slacks and peach angora sweater, clinging to the packages.

"Quick, Chloe, I'm dropping them."

"Well, you didn't need to carry so many at once!" responded Chloe, "Put them in the sitting room," (which was now officially the larger front room).

"Odd you should call it that," said Joel, "since there's no place to sit." He dropped his boxes to the floor. "Some people, I suppose not everybody, I don't know, but I'd guess that some people put furniture in there apartments. Ever considered such a thing?"

"Gloria, Chloe had lately slipped into calling her mother Gloria, since everyone else did, Gloria says we don't need much because we don't have anyone to visit us. She also says that when we have a house we can get furniture."

"Well, you tell Gloria that I intend to visit more often so she needs to buy a couple of chairs or a couch or something. If I'm going to stop by while she and Harold go to dinner (you are not old enough to be left alone), I suggest she get me a chair."

"We can go to my room and you can sit on my bed." suggested Chloe.

"Thanks, Chloe, but I'm holding out for a couch and possibly a coffee table. In the meantime, let's pull the kitchen table and chairs out here. We have work to do!"

With table and chairs in place, he opened the first box.

"What do you think of this?" he asked. "Want to try it on or shall I. I bought six styles for the store and I haven't even looked at them yet."

He set the first wig, a softly curled, shoulder length, auburn piece on the table.

"Let's take them all out and put them on the table first. You know that I have no idea how to put one of these things on, don't you?" said Chloe.

"And why would you, Little One? Because you have beautiful, thick, shiny dark hair. Ah... what I would give to have your hair."

Chloe smiled. Joel always made Chloe smile. They chatted while they unboxed the wigs.

"You know, Joel, I've spent a fair amount of time in waiting rooms reading psychology magazines and..."

"How's that?" interrupted Joel. As he put up the large mirror in place.

"You know...I had to take Gloria to her appointments for awhile... Anyway, the magazines say that kids need a father figure, or at least a male role model of some kind, to look up to. Someone kind and with a strong moral character. They recommend someone in a loving relationship with their partner. So, is it OK if you're my father figure?"

"So, he was that bad was he?"

"Yes, he was. But you're great. You're all those good things and you and Marten are really nice to each other...and you're always nice to me."

"Promise not to call me Dad?"

"Promise. I don't *want* you to be my dad."

"Then, I accept the position. I'll do my best. I'll start by showing you how to put on a wig. These are actually quite nice."

During this entire conversation, Joel and Chloe had been unwrapping wigs and setting them across the table.

"Very nice." said Joel as they stood back and had a good look.

"Are they? I don't know how to tell," said Chloe.

"Well, first of all, I only bought human hair; no yak, no wool, no synthetics."

"That's disgusting," said Chloe.

"Try not to think about it. These two are hand-tied into a lace cap. It makes them look very realistic. Those four are hand tied into a lace front only cap; it makes them a little less expensive and a little more durable. These are all display models. Each wig we sell needs to be specifically measured for the person who wants to buy it. It seems that I ordered four of these in my size, what a coincidence. One I ordered in Marten's size, and this cute little honey-colored, bob-styled one just happens to be in your size."

He pulled out a chair. "Have a seat."

As Chloe sat down, her face brushed against Joel's sweater. She could see him in the mirror all orange and peach. His cheeks glowed from his own reflection.

"You look especially nice tonight," said Chloe. "That sweater is sooo soft. I've never felt anything so soft."

"Thanks. Marten is picking me up later, when he's done studying. We can talk sweaters later; wigs now. Pay attention."

Joel's hands worked quickly. Once the wig was in place and lightly styled, he moved on to make-up. He turned Chloe's chair around and set to work. They talked girl talk; skin tones, nail polish, earrings, bone structure, etc...

"Actually you should probably put the makeup on first, then the wig," said Joel, "but this works for now, if we're careful."

When he was done, he pulled Chloe's chair back around so she could see herself in the mirror.

"That's not really me!" said Chloe. "How did you do that. I look pretty."

"You know exactly how I did it. I told you everything while I was doing it. Of course, you look pretty. You always look pretty. But this would be for special occasions, like going to the dance with Jeff."

"Who's Jeff"

"I don't know. He's just an example. Isn't there somebody you have you're eye on?"

Chloe blushed.

"Ah Ha! There is somebody!"

And then they talked boys. Who was this "not Jeff" person? How did you meet him? How did you meet Marten? How old is he ? How old were you? What did you talk about?

"What do you mean he doesn't talk to you? We'll fix that. This weekend I am taking you and your mother shopping. Furniture for her. Angora sweater for you."

"I can't wear an angora sweater. "

"You must if it's a gift. What color are we looking for?

"Blue," said Chloe, instantly, thinking of St. Cecilia's.

"So you were listening. Blue will go beautifully with your coloring. Green would also work, especially with your green eyes. "

"Blue," repeated Chloe.

"Blue then. So, there you have it. Blue angora sweater. But there are rules that come with angora, especially for someone who is ten years old."

Marten showed up just as Joel reached rule number five, the one regarding boys hands. Joel was more than a little relieved. Gloria and Harold were late.

"Better make yourself comfortable." said Chloe. "I've never known her to be on time."

Marten sat down at the table and Chloe fit him with a wig cap, just as Joel had showed her. Then she slid on a long, black curly wig. It had been given some loft on top and a nice layered cut throughout. Chloe looped one side up behind Marten's ear and held it in place with a tortoise shell clip.

Chloe and Joel *oohed* and *aahed* and they all went into the bathroom to admire the three of them together, totem pole style, in the full length mirror behind the door. Then, they packed everything into the car and Marten said, "OK, now I'm starving. We have to go, Chloe."

"No, we don't" countered Joel, " We are not leaving her all alone."

"Hi, I'm home," announced Gloria, as she came in the door.

"First time's funny, second time's silly, third time's a spanking," said Marten, "Unless you like that sort of thing, in which case we will think of something else. Don't be late again. We gotta run. Smooches all around."

28
THE COST OF RESCUE

Chloe reached the park just as the school bus turned the corner and headed downhill. She sat on a bench and considered her options; none of them good. She could ask Gloria for a ride to school...almost laughable. She could skip school and take a field trip to the public library...almost plausible. She could ask for help...almost do-able. She could go home before Gloria went to work and confess all...unthinkable.

She went down the list again. Asking Gloria for a ride was the same as confessing and Chloe's entire world would go up in flames. If she skipped school, Sister Mary Katherine would look for Chloe's non-existent file; again flames. So who could she call? The only person she knew with a car... Joel. Besides, this was what a father figure was supposed to do, rescue the daughter figure from the evil hordes.

She could see Joel's car still parked on the other side of the block. She ran as if the hounds of hell were at her heels, and threw herself on the hood, just as Joel and Marten came out of the apartment building.

"Joel, I know you are not my father but you are a good man." She stood up and looked him in the eyes. "A good, good man. And a kind man," she said. "Save me."

"Everybody in the car," said Joel, "We have to get Marten to work. Then, to the best of my abilities, Chloe, I will save you. Just sit tight."

"Marten, you never saw me, promise?" insisted Chloe as Marten climbed out of the car. "Promise me."

Marten hesitated.

"Promise her, Marten, you're going to be late."

"OK. Promise." He gave Joel a peck on the cheek.

Joel turned to Chloe, "I'm going to miss work aren't I ?"

"Yes, I believe you are," said Chloe. "Just keep driving. We're going over the bridge."

"Road trip. This sounds like fun. What's up, Chloe?"

"I missed my bus. I need a ride to school."

"Did I miss something?'

"Yes," said Chloe, and she explained. The legion of those in cahoots was rapidly expanding. Chloe couldn't even count them all.

When he dropped her off at the school grounds, Sister Mary Katherine waved at them both from the front steps. Joel waved back.

"Your father looks like such a nice man," she said.

"Yes," responded Chloe, as she slipped around the corner of the building, thinking 'Into the Valley of Death rode the six hundred', or maybe just twelve or fifteen; I haven't counted lately."

At the end of the day, before they shuffled her onto the bus, Chloe spoke to her minions. She feared for their well being, She feared the wrath of the headmistress. She wanted to protect those who had protected her. She explained to them all the importance of the protection of confessional.

Suddenly the entire ridership of bus 12 became extremely pious. The father barely had time for his lunch. As soon as the noon bell rang there was a waiting line for the confessional. The father finally posted a sign up sheet. Sister Mary Katherine congratulated him on his success in drawing the children to a more righteous life.

Father Ignatius was only too happy to accept the compliment. He urged the children to expand their Chloe Club confessions to resemble something similar to the real thing. It worked, to some degree. It became clear, however, that no one was actually repentant, which made it difficult for him to promise the Lord's forgiveness.

He did, however, strongly suggest that the Lord would look favorably on those who joined St. Cecelia's choir.

St. Cecelia is the patron saint of music and Father Ignatius longed for a choir. He, himself, was a strong baritone and missed being surrounded by voices in unison. His chapel was small and could not provide the booming voice of an organ, but it had a good piano and he, the music teacher, was a fine pianist. Together they pulled together St. Cecelia's first choir. Practice was scheduled three times a day, twice a week, to ensure that all the students from Bus 12 could attend.

Since nearly all the choir members were on Bus 12, the ride to and from school became a traveling concert, in four part harmony. Even the bus driver began singing along. The students arrived at school feeling uplifted and the bus driver continued his day humming "Nearer My God to Thee". Life was good, except for Joel.

Joel was in a quandary. Gloria was his best friend, after Marten of course. Chloe trusted him implicitly. Stuck between Scylla and Charybdis, Joel's next few days were tainted with feelings of guilt and deception.

After just one week Marten noticed a change. Joel was not his usual carefree self. He was brooding and had lost his normally lighthearted attitude.

"Joel, what are you so worried about," asked Marten. "Are you overdrawn at the bank again? Did you put a dent in the car? Did you put a dent in someone else's car? You are still insured, aren't you? Honestly, Joel, it can't be all that bad. We can work it out. Talk to me."

Joel talked. Marten listened. And now Marten was in cahoots.

29
JUDGEMENT DAY

City of Paris was giving Gloria a promotion. She was soon to be the assistant manager of the jewelry department even thou she now only worked part time, City of Paris liked her. She had been instructed to arrive at work by 8:30 am to learn her new duties, which included handling money at the beginning and ending of each day and the opening and closing of the department when required.

"Hurry up, Chloe," Gloria, shouted from the bathroom. "I want you at the bus stop before I grab the cable car for work.

Ordinarily Gloria was not required to start her shift until 10:00 am. She took lunch at 1:00 and left work at 6:00. It was a long day, but it gave her the luxury of waking up slowly and getting Chloe off to school while she was still in relatively good humor. Gloria checked her make-up one last time and headed out the door not long after Chloe. As the cable car passed Huntington Park, she turned just in time to watch Chloe board Saint Cecelia's school bus , the bus she had never seen on her old schedule. As the bus pulled forward Chloe just caught a glimpse of her mother's jaw drop. Ballanchine could not have choreographed the incident more perfectly. Mother and daughter, both horrified, were carried their separate ways, each with a terrible image scorched into their brains.

Chloe spent a confusing day at school. There was a certain relief in being found out. A heavy burden had been lifted from her shoulders. Her studies suffered, however. She kept wondering what Napa Valley was like; whether or not a young girl such as she could survive on the contents of tide pools; whether or not Mrs. Fitz would be so glad to see her that she would invite her to live with her...no questions asked.

She went for study time with Father Ignatius but walked rudely past him and directly into the confessional.

"Forgive me Father, for I have sinned. It has been one day since my last confession." It had always been one day since her last confession, except on Mondays, when it was three days. The confession had always been the same, but not today. "Father," said Chloe, "this is a proactive confession for something I haven't done yet. I probably won't be able to get back to you after I do this thing." Tears came to her eyes. "I will either run away or I will be dead, because if I go home tonight my mother will surely kill me," she sobbed.

"Chloe, what has happened to upset you so. Surely, we can fix it."

"Not unless you can erase my mother's memory. She saw me get on the bus this morning."

In his mind, the father said, "Holy crap!"

After a short pause he said, "Well, this does appear to pose some difficulties."

"Twelve Hail Marys is not going to do the trick, Father," said Chloe, pointing out the obvious.

She explained Napa Valley, tide pools, and Mrs. Fitz to the Father. "What do you think?"

"Well, Chloe," he said, "you know that if you do any of those things God will always be by your side, but so will the police. Mrs. Fitz will go to jail for kidnapping and your mother's heart will be broken. You will also spend many cold and hungry nights before they actually find you, so let's think of something else."

Chloe didn't want to be cold and hungry. She was willing to consider alternatives.

It was some time before Chloe went back to her biology book. In that time she agreed that going back home was the best course of action. She should think less about herself, said Father, and more about her mother. Father Ignatius suggested, in particular, that Chloe might consider making her mother feel less as if she had lost control of the situation, though she had; less frightened, though she was; and convince her that a positive outcome for all could be reached if she and her mother just worked together.

"He's kidding himself," thought Chloe but she was too polite to say so. Then she thought of how she had taken her mother to the psychiatrist, how she had taken her mother shopping, how she had picked her mother up in the dessert and driven them to San Francisco. She could save herself and her mother, too. She had done it before. She pulled her Supergirl cape out of the cobwebs and threw it over her shoulders. Once again she would save the day.

Because of her new, earlier shift, Gloria was home in time to meet Chloe at the bus stop. She decided against making a scene in public. Instead, when Chloe walked in the door, her mother was already seated at the kitchen table, waiting for her. Chloe was forced to squeeze past her in order to reach her own bedroom.

"It's called lying by omission, Chloe. You are NOT allowed to lie to your mother. Put your books down, get an orange soda, and join me." Gloria thought about that for a second, "How do you even *have* books?"

Gloria had bought herself a canned Manhattan at the nearby liquor store before she reached home. It was not something she usually did, but she was trying to avoid a long prison sentence for child abuse.

When Chloe did not appear at the table Gloria began wishing she had bought more Manhattans. "Now!" she said.

Chloe sat.

"How long did you think you could get away with this?!"

The conversation had already begun with exclamation marks. "Not a good sign," thought Chloe.

"I was hoping forever," she replied truthfully, "but I guess that was impractical."

"Impractical? Impractical?! This is insane!!! What am I going to do with you??" It was a question mothers have been asking since time immemorial.

"Send me to St. Cecilia's," replied Chloe, trying to sound cheerful without being too flip.

Cheerful was good. Gloria really needed cheerful.

"I could send you to college for what it would cost to send you to that school."

That's what Annie's dad said."

"Well, he can probably afford it. What does HE do?"

"He's an ambassador."

"Seriously?"

"Seriously," respond Chloe. "And now that you know all this can I go spend Saturday afternoon at her house? She lives just up the hill at the Fairmont."

"She *lives* at the Fairmont?!" Gloria took a breath. "I think, perhaps, you will still be grounded on Saturday. And don't change the subject."

There followed Chloe's epic saga of life in the bamboo, her friendship with Annie and Evelyn, and her introduction to Father Ignatius. She explained her manipulation of the confessional, acceptance (in good standing) by teachers and students alike, and her ability to maintain a fictitious "A" average through hard work, perseverance, tutoring and deceit.

Gloria was filled with both horror and admiration. "Only my daughter could have pulled that off," slipped out of her mouth before she could stop herself.

Chloe smiled. "This is not going so badly," she thought. So she said "Let's go shopping tomorrow. I want to buy a skirt, and I'd love to see were you work." She quickly added, with feigned humility, "If that's OK with you."

"Game, set, match!" thought Chloe. She had been watching the tennis classes at St. Cecelia's.

But she had played that move too soon.

"Close but no cigar," thought Gloria.

"Again," said Gloria angrily. "Don't change the subject."

However, Gloria was momentarily distracted. "Shopping? Skirt? See where I work?" She felt a little off balance. After all, she did want to go shopping.

"Chloe, in light of your considerable, though seriously dangerous, bravery and creativity, coupled with the fact that this is the first time I have ever known you to have friends, I would love to send you to St. Cecelia's. You are certainly smart enough and I think you deserve it, really I do. Just tell me how to do it."

"Well, I've been thinking about that for a while, but I could hardly ask you before now," said Chloe.

Their discussion went on for another 15 minutes before they agreed on a plan. A weak plan, but it was the best they could do. Then they went across the street to the Vietnamese restaurant for dinner, where they planned a Saturday shopping trip. Game set match after all.

The following day was a Thursday. Chloe was ordered to stay home. Theoretically speaking, it was the first day of several years of being grounded. Practically speaking, she was home because her mother was on the phone to Father Ignatius. Then she was on the phone to the headmistress of St. Cecelia's. Then she was calling Marten.

Headmistress Sister Mary Katherine instructed Chloe to report to school as usual and go to the library. If there was any hope at all for her to attend St. Cecelia's, she must take the entrance exams.

Saturday morning at nine o'clock, Marten drove up in a car from the lot where he worked so that a 'possible customer' could take a test drive. Marten, Gloria and Chloe headed across the Golden Gate Bridge (a first for Gloria), through Mill Valley and up the side of Mount Tamalpais to St. Cecelia's Catholic School.

They went directly to the chapel. Chloe skipped the confessional. What was the point? The father provided tea in the presbytery while they discussed the problem. Then he prayed for them. They would need it, he said. The headmistress was not a push over.

They all proceeded to Sister Mary Katherine's office with their appeal. It was hard for Sister Mary Katherine to be terribly stern with Chloe. She had liked Chloe from the moment she had met her. She had to admit that the child already had a favorable history at the school, the teachers and students liked her, and her ardent desire to attend was unquestionable. Nevertheless, she had behaved very badly in her deceitful ways. She had involved other students in her deceit, and she had seriously abused the use of the sanctity of the confessional in order to manipulate Father.

"Judgement is the Lord's alone," reminded Father Ignatius. "She needs us. That much is obvious." Somewhere in his speech he threw in a little of the 23rd Psalm, "surely goodness and *mercy* will follow me all the days of my life", and further on he added "suffer the little children and forbid them not, to come to me; for such is the kingdom of heaven. Mathew 19:14." By the time he was done there was not a dry eye in the house, except for Sister Mary Katherine's.

"I will take it to the board," she promised. "But you must report to the library tomorrow morning and take the entrance exams."

The visitors said their "goodbyes" and piled back into the car.

"No problem, then," commented Marten.

The others glared at him in silence.

Sister Mary Katherine took Chloe's plight to the board of directors, who immediately said "No". Then Sister Mary Katherine handed them Chloe's test scores. Their eyes lit up. All of them. The board was a very competitive lot. It was the goal of every last one of them to beat St. Francis' School in Point Reyes in every academic competition on the calendar and then go on to the state competition. Chloe suddenly glowed with a pure, white, heavenly light.

"But we can't be that transparent," said one.

'She's a bad egg," announced another.

"This year's scholarship money has already been awarded," said another with regret.

"There may be more scholarship money than you think," said Felicity Windemere, President of the Board. Her daughter talked about Chloe all the time. She credited Chloe and her friend Evelyn with keeping her daughter out of reform school. "And she certainly is not a 'bad egg'! That's just ridiculous."

"Lucy Schroeder is on scholarship," she continued," and is leaving at the end of term. Her father got transferred to Oklahoma City. I think, that in light of the situation, you could convince other donors to pitch in until those funds are available." She preferred not to refer to herself in the third person, but it sounded acceptable under the circumstances.

∞

On Monday Chloe dressed for school as she had always done, in a pair of slacks and a white blouse with her borrowed skirt tucked up under her borrowed blazer, which due to the early November weather, was hidden under a light jacket. Although everyone knew of her ruse, she was afraid to change her habits or her dress for fear it would be bad luck and affect the outcome of her today's meeting. She had been summoned to Sister Mary Katherine's office at 11 o'clock to hear the school board's official ruling regarding her presence at St. Cecelia's.

She boarded the bus and went directly to the window seat in the far back, which she had come to consider her personal corner. She slipped her skirt down and her slacks off. Annie was waiting for her.

"Oh, my gosh, Chloe, today's the day, isn't it." Chloe just looked at her. Annie squeezed her hand and scooted to the opposite corner of the back seat. "You're nervous," said Annie. "At least I would be. I'll leave you alone."

She kept talking. She was Annie, she couldn't help herself. She scooted back to Chloe's side and continued, "What if this doesn't go your way, what's the back-up plan? What am I saying, of course they'll let you in. How could they resist you. I'm not helping am I?" She slid back to the far window.

"Come back," said Chloe. "I have no backup plan. This has to work. Just don't talk about it. I feel like throwing up."

"Well don't do it on me," said Annie. And they both laughed. Then they were quiet for most of the trip to school.

Upon arrival Chloe went straight to the chapel. "Forgive me father for I have sinned. It has been four days since my last confession."

"Yes Chloe?"

"I used you just like Sister Mary Katherine said I did. I'm sorry. Can I be just sort of sorry? Because if I hadn't done that I would have missed out on everything I've done for the past month. I wouldn't have known Evy and Annie and especially you. So I'm only sorry about putting you on the spot. The rest as great. And since I may never see you again I just want to say thanks." And she started to cry.

"OK. OK. You're forgiven. Say ten Hail Marys. We have to get you a rosary. And I wasn't on the spot. It's my job. Now, can we go sit in the vestry and have tea, I have something for you."

Father Ignatius made a lovely cup of Irish Breakfast tea for each of them, though Chloe's was a bit weaker. He put some biscuits on the table. Then he put some packages and a note in front of her.

"I was supposed to wait until after lunch to give these to you but I think you need them now. Don't let anyone know that I let the cat out of the bag. Pretend it's all a surprise to you. Now open, open, open."

First she read the letter:

Chloe Dear,

I am so happy for you. You deserve this scholarship. I hope you are as happy about it as I am. Wear these and shine.

Love,

Mrs. Fitz.

"Come in," said Sister Mary Katherine. She was standing in the window with the light streaming beatifically down on her. "I imagine you have already been to the chapel to see Father Ignatius. He never could keep a secret. Congratulations Chloe, and welcome."

"Thank you," was all Chloe could say.

Sister Mary Katherine was very calm and reserved. She glided back to her desk. Chloe was in awe of her. She handed Chloe some papers.

"Here is your schedule," she said simply. "Due to a teacher's workshop, there is no school for the rest of the week. When you get back on Monday, I'm sure Evelyn and Anna Claire will help you find your way around. On Monday you can wear your own uniform. It was very thoughtful of Mrs. Fitz to provide it. Be sure you send her a thank you note right away."

"One more thing. You broke a lot of rules to get into this school. If you break any more you will be out in an instant."

"Yes, Sister. Thank you, Sister."

"You are not here because we admire rule breakers. You are here, primarily, because the world needs fine minds, and you, Chloe, have one. Don't let us down. Go out there and use it well." Then she flashed Chloe her beautiful smile and Chloe smiled back.

30

LOOSE ENDS

Chloe and Mrs. Fitz sat at the garden table sipping a mild, Japanese green tea and recovering from a short but intense outbreak of tears. They were happy tears, if there is such a thing. Happy tears always contain a remembrance of the sadness that preceded them. Happy, however, persevered and by the time Mihana allowed Evelyn to join them they were all smiles. Together they looked at the photo album made from the photos Chloe had helped take.

Harold and Gloria were taking a Sunday drive up the coast highway. They hoped to spot some grey whales for Harold to photograph from a distance. Later in the week he would hire a boat to take him for some close up shots. Gloria was not invited on that trip. Grey whales are generally not aggressive but can, even in the process of ignoring you, cause some serious damage simply by virtue of their hugeness, up to 35 tons according to Harold. Harold wanted to get very close to them. Gloria was relieved to be staying home. When they dropped Chloe at Evelyn's, they promised to be back around three.

Mihana provided a picnic and, after the reunion, they all went down to the beach for an hour or so. Chloe, Evelyn and Evelyn's dad walked down the hill and over the road to Muir Beach. Mrs. Fitz rode there with Mihana.

Chloe had to stand and absorb the immensity of the ocean before she could even begin to consider exploring tide pools and rock outcrops. It was her first day at a beach, any beach. She had never even been to Lake Michigan. The most water she had ever seen in one place was the water in the inflatable pool in her back yard in

Chicago. Here she could smell the ocean...taste it in the air...feel it on her face. Long rows of waves tumbled over each other in their race to the shore, then sank into the sand at her feet, or slid back under the rows and rows of waves that had been chasing them. The rushing sound was loud and incessant. The grey skies were reflected in the greyer water. Chloe was not ready to say that she loved the ocean. It was frightening and overwhelming.

"Don't leave her side for a second," her father told Evelyn. "Don't even let her go wading. It's too cold today anyway, but remind her. Don't let her do anything risky. Don't forget, she can't swim a stroke."

Evelyn was happy to explain rip tides, undertow, and tides in general to Chloe. At that point Chloe had no desire to go in the water at all, ever, especially after Evelyn schooled her in the migration pattern of the great white shark.

"This is definitely not a swimming beach," explained Evelyn. "Now let me show you what we can do."

The two ran down to the north end of the cove and into the rock outcrop.

"The tide is out now," said Evelyn. "You wouldn't want to be trapped over here after the tide starts back in. You couldn't make it up that cliff behind us to get to safety." She sat on a rock with her feet wide apart and looked down between her knees into the shallow water trapped below with the smaller rocks and sand.

Chloe perched on a rock across from her. "Thank God I didn't decide to run away and live on things I found in tide pools." She almost gagged at just the thought.

Below her in the smushy, stranded black-green sea weed were some small squishy anemones with tentacles waving in the water. Evy touched one and it sucked all it's tentacles back into it's body, lickity-split. Chloe tried this and the tentacles disappeared. She was about to try it again when a rock, no, a small starfish, moved. She couldn't have been more surprised. Evelyn was looking for a starfish for her tank but this one was to big.

"Besides," she said, "I already have an orange one like that. Tell me when you find one that looks different."

They rose and climbed over to another pool. There were mussels stuck to the rocks.

"You can eat these," explained Evelyn. "They're really delicious. My mom will make us some sometime."

Suddenly, the clouds spread and the sun showed itself. Blue skies and the warmth of the sun changed everything. When Chloe sat up to take off her sweater, the world around her was entirely different. The ocean had gone from grey to blue to match the sky. Children on the beach were laughing and giggling. Adults were leaving their cars to play with their children. The fog had burned off.

Evelyn and Chloe ran down the beach at top speed until they could run no more. They fell to their knees laughing. Too out of breath to jump up, they made sand angels and decorated them with seaweed hair and shell eyes. They brushed the sand off each other and ran back to Mr. Fitz, who put down his cane to engage them in a game of keepaway with the waves. Arm in arm the girls danced around him singing, "by the sea, by the sea, by the beautiful sea...."

Mr. Fitz proved to be an exceptional skipper of rocks and finder of tiny things; moon snails, cone shells, purple dwarf olives, and small pieces of colored glass, tumbled and polished by the waves. They spread their collection on the picnic blanket for the Mrs. Fitzes to admire. They, too, had been coaxed from the car when the sun came out, and the picnic basket was overflowing on the blanket. When the last sandwich had disappeared and the last muffin had been consumed, they all rode up the hill together.

When Gloria and Harold arrived to pick up Chloe, they found the girls back in the gardens. There were two separate gardens, side by side, with a walkway and the table between them. The older Mrs. Fitz's garden was a cottage garden adjusted to the seaside climate. It contained roses of different hues, blue rosemary, deep purple lavender, indigo cat mint and white Lily of the Nile. Blue lily of the Nile stood tall throughout the rose ribbed sea kale. The huge blue flowers of late season artichokes were displayed over the plants' extraordinary leaves. Mrs. Fitz enjoyed different combinations of colors at different times of year. When her perennials were not blooming she bought pots of blooming specimens from a nearby nursery. She also chose new specimens not only for their colors but for the texture of their petals and leaves. She still enjoyed cutting flowers for the house.

The younger Mrs. Fitz's garden was a traditional Japanese Zen garden. It primarily contained carefully placed rocks of varying sizes, mosses, and fine sandwich was frequently raked. The garden's purpose was not to stimulate one's emotions with form and color, but to stimulate meditation through abstract simplicity. Instead of cutting flowers and shaping bushes, the Japanese gardener rakes the sand into rivers, lakes or simply textural shapes. Chloe and Evelyn were raking the garden into ocean waves when Harold drove up.

Gloria found the Fitzes very likable and the feeling was mutual, considering the brevity of the encounter. Everyone smiled and waved and the visitors headed back towards San Francisco.

"Please can we stop at school for a minute," Chloe asked.

"What for ?" asked Gloria, who was getting tired and wanted to go home.

"I want to talk to Father Ignatius for a few minutes. It won't take long."

"It's not really very late," said Harold, who liked Chloe and wanted her to like him. We can wait in the car."

"Well, actually you can't," thought Chloe but she decided to leave that part out.

During one of her daily confessions she had told Father Ignatius something new. She confessed that she had stolen one of the pictures of Hal from her mother's purse. The confessional was occupied for quite some time that day, not so much because of the stealing issue, which merited twelve Hail Marys, but because of the "'whose Hal?" issue, which Chloe had never spoken to anyone about before. After that they had had a few more talks about Hal, in the vestry, some times with cookies and milk. The father was waiting for Chloe and Gloria to show up that afternoon.

When they parked at St. Cecelia's they all got out to stretch their legs. Chloe asked her mother to come in with her. She was going to light a candle for Hal.

Gloria said, "No, Chloe, I don't want to." Chloe knew there was no preparing her for this, so she had sprung it on her out of nowhere.

"It's a way for us to remember him without talking," said Chloe. "Please do this for me. It will only take a minute."

"Who's Hal?" wondered Harold, but he kept his mouth shut. This seemed not the time to ask.

The chapel appeared dark after a day outdoors. The darkness made Gloria feel instantly tired. This was one of the only times she wasn't glad to be entering a church. The other time she wanted to run out was Hal's funeral, something she never wanted to think about again. Yet here she was.

The chapel was small, built to seat only as many boarding students as attended the school over the weekends. During the week only a small portion of the student body attended prayers at any given time. There were only five rows of pews on each side of the aisle. Colored light streamed in from a small stained glass window at the end of each row. The windows were without subject and contained only multiple square panes of colored glass. Between each pew, therefore between each small window, was an enclave containing the statue of a saint with her or his name and significance posted beneath. A truly calm and beautiful window filled the wall behind the alter, where Mary cradled the baby Jesus in her arms. Gloria was relieved not to be overwhelmed by majestic surroundings. She cried softly, but only for a moment.

The confessional was in the back, only a few steps inside the door. Towards the front of the church, just to the left of the pulpit, stood a narrow rectangular table. A long, three-tiered, metal candle holder stood on the table with a box of four inch tapers by its side.

Chloe and Gloria stood facing the Madonna and Child. Chloe put two coins on the table, handed her mother a candle, and took one for herself. They put the candles in the holder and lit them.

"For Hal," whispered Chloe.

Gloria then turned to Harold, who was still standing quietly in the doorway.

"You, too, Harold," she said. "It's your turn."

Harold walked up to the candles and whispered to Gloria, "But I don't even know who Hal is."

Gloria pulled one of Hal's pictures from her purse. "This is Hal. He's my son. He is part of us. So now you know." She put a coin on the table and handed Harold a candle. Harold lit the candle while Father Ignatius said a prayer. They thanked the father.

"See you Monday," Chloe said as they left.

"Always full of surprises, you two," said Harold as they got back into the car. Chloe immediately pulled out her note cards. She thought this might be a good time to move the conversation along.

"Did you know that if a starfish looses an arm it can grow it back?"

"Where did you learn that?" asked Harold, thinking Chloe might have the right idea.

"Evelyn taught me all about tide pools today." Then she pulled out her card on tides. She had jotted down a few things Evelyn had told her on the beach.

Harold seemed to know a bit about tides and the conversation took on a pleasant life of it's own. Gloria remained quiet for a while but when the talk turned to great white sharks, she joined in, mostly in dismay.

Chloe mentioned that you could eat mussels from the pools and that you just needed lemon and garlic and some good bread.

"Too bad I don't cook," said Harold.

"Neither do we," added Gloria .

"Well, one of us had better learn then," chimed in Chloe.

31

TRIUMPHANT

Besides stopping at Huntington Park, Bus 12 now stopped on Polk Street, upon request, right in front of GLORY. The driver swung the door open for Chloe, who looked out for a moment with one hand on the railing, before slowly putting forth her right foot to feel down for the next step. She didn't run down the steps like most of the other kids. She took her time, relishing every moment, descending like Miss Universe having just accepted the crown.

Chloe wore no crown, but what she did wear was just as significant. Her right foot emerged from the bus exposing the gleaming white of her new tennis shoes followed by her white cotton knee socks. She paused, then glided down to the second step revealing her perfect 10-year-old knee peeking out from beneath the hem of her very own navy blue, pleated skirt. Her long sleeved Windsor white blouse with the buttoned down collar was partly hidden by the navy blue, cotton blazer that hung unbuttoned down the front. What was different about the outfit she wore today as opposed to the one she had worn last week? Two very significant things: inside each piece of clothing was a label reading Chloe S, St. Cecilia's ; also, it was not stuffed in a Jade Garden shopping bag for the trip home, she was still wearing it proudly when she got off the bus. She hopped from the bus's third step to the street, where she stood with a new attitude. Her heavily laden book bag swung specifically from her right shoulder so no one could miss the gold emblem of her school emblazoned on her left breast pocket.

Academic scholarship. She loved the sound of it. It was about her, not about her mother's behavior, or her mother's money, or her mother's anything. She earned her place because of who *she* was. They wanted Chloe because of *her* record, *her* abilities, and the way *she* thought. This had never happened before. As a result, there had probably never been a child so full of school spirit as Chloe was. In a moment of unbridled enthusiasm she pictured herself as a cheerleader but snapped out of it immediately, wondering what she could possibly be thinking.

The bus pulled away exposing her back to the warmth of the mid-November sun. She freed her hair from the confines of the tortoise shell clip and tossed it the way Joel had taught her. She looked above the storefront before her at the three foot script that read "*Glory*" in bold italics.

Her book bag was digging into her shoulder but she didn't mind. It was filled with books and notebooks whose margins overflowed with Chloe's additions to the text. Her notes included, but were not limited to, small flocks of ravens being overcome by bats of all sizes and shapes. The ravens, who were meekly calling out, "Nevermore," were having a hard time holding their own as the bats swooped through page after page whispering, "Forevermore." The battle was not yet over but the odds were definitely favoring the bats.

Joel was unpacking clothing. He felt it was his responsibility to try on a sample of everything, just to make sure the quality was that which he had expected. The actual grand opening was coming up and Joel wanted everything to be perfect. Since Chloe had come clean ,his conscious was also clear and he was enjoying himself, thoroughly.

Joel was working on the display for stylish young men in well put together attire for the office. They might be architects working at their tables or bank officers at their desks. They might possibly be clothing store owners such as himself. It could be appropriate attire for a man climbing the corporate ladder by day who would change, in the evening, into something less formal and more feminine from the other side of the store. This was a display for the 'men's clothing' side of the store. Gay or straight, Joel knew how to dress.

When Chloe walked in the door, Joel was admiring himself in the mirror.

"Looking good," said Chloe, who couldn't wipe the grin off her face.

Without turning around he asked "Do I look straight?"

"You're far too beautiful to look straight," replied Chloe.

"Why, thank you Princess," he said. "Gloria," he shouted up the stairs, "watch the store, I am taking your daughter for ice cream."

Then he turned and saw Chloe. "Well, look at you, Miss Academic Scholarship to a Private School. Very impressive. I'd say we both look beautiful. Shall we go?" and he offered her his arm. She laughed and they left.

Once outside, Chloe stopped for a just a moment. She stood there measuring the thinness of the air at sea level. It wasn't all that thin. She was having no trouble breathing at all. Nevertheless, she was soaring. She and her mother had taken the road less traveled only to find that others had, too. San Francisco was the crossroads for the roads less traveled. It was the Grand Central Station for the roads less traveled.

When they returned, Gloria was standing outside with Harold, who had stopped by to say "'hello". Joel relaxed up against the building next to Harold. Marten waved from the upstairs window. Gloria leaned up against her sparkling new, white, 1963 Pontiac GTO convertible with the red interior. She pulled Chloe over in front of her and let her arms fall loosely across her daughter's chest. The move was not staged or choreographed in any way. It was done out of warmth and affection.

"So now that you're a successful, independent San Francisco business woman...Gloria...will you marry me?" asked Harold.

"Not this year, laughed Gloria. "Maybe next year."

He knew she meant it.

She knew he meant it to.

EPILOGUE

The following year Marten and Joel moved to the Castro district and opened a second Glory, leaving Gloria to manage the first. Shortly after that, the partners celebrated the opening of the LA Glory, followed closely behind by the N.Y. and the London stores. Gloria, Marten and Joel found themselves mentioned in the 1964 edition of *Life* magazine, which featured San Francisco as the gay capitol of the nation.

Gloria, Chloe and Harold bought a home in Pacific Heights with fantastic views of the Bay. They bought furniture. Harold was persistent and finally coaxed Gloria into an outdoor marriage in Golden Gate Park. Gloria hired their friend Susan to manage the Polk Street store and spent less and less time with the day to day business of Glory. This gave her more and more time to travel with Harold. While he focused on nature photography, she gathered textile samples and photographed native dress from around the world.

Chloe and Evelyn attended Berkeley and Anna Claire went to Stanford. Sometime in her sophomore year, Chloe succumbed to the siren call of San Francisco in the 60's and took a break from school. She spent one memorable weekend laying on the floor of her Haight-Ashbury apartment while ravens and bats swooped about dressed in tiny pairs of red, blue, and green corduroy pants and Grace Slick would not stop singing. Chloe did not wish to be a volunteer for America, she just wanted to go to sleep. When the walls stopped moving she packed her bags and hastened gratefully back to school. She graduated with honors and accepted a teaching position at St. Cecelia's. After two years she went to graduate school and became a professor of religious studies.

Made in the USA
Columbia, SC
07 January 2025